W9-DHH-240

"I suppose you're here to arrest me for the illegal adoption?"

"That all depends."

"On what?" Finally, there was a slip in her resolve. Her voice cracked.

"You." Luke came to a stop in front of the house, turned off the engine and stared at her.

"This is my babysitter's house. What are we doing here?"

He turned toward Elaina so he could see every nuance of her reaction. He ignored how beautiful, how vulnerable she looked. "Why do you think I'm here?"

"Oh, no. I can't let you do this. You can't arrest me. You don't understand—he's my son. I'm the only mother he's ever known."

"Believe me, I know that."

"I won't let you take him from me," she insisted.

"You have no choice."

"Then I need to talk to his father, make him understand how much Christopher means to me."

"You're already talking to him. Christopher is *my* son."

DELORES FOSSEN

UNDERCOVER DADDY

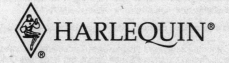

HARLEQUIN®

TORONTO • NEW YORK • LONDON
AMSTERDAM • PARIS • SYDNEY • HAMBURG
STOCKHOLM • ATHENS • TOKYO • MILAN • MADRID
PRAGUE • WARSAW • BUDAPEST • AUCKLAND

If you purchased this book without a cover you should be aware
that this book is stolen property. It was reported as "unsold and
destroyed" to the publisher, and neither the author nor the
publisher has received any payment for this "stripped book."

To Daphne Betterton. You're the best.

ISBN-13: 978-0-373-69257-6
ISBN-10:   0-373-69257-9

UNDERCOVER DADDY

Copyright: © 2007 by Delores Fossen

All rights reserved. Except for use in any review, the reproduction or
utilization of this work in whole or in part in any form by any electronic,
mechanical or other means, now known or hereafter invented, including
xerography, photocopying and recording, or in any information storage
or retrieval system, is forbidden without the written permission of the
publisher, Harlequin Enterprises Limited, 225 Duncan Mill Road,
Don Mills, Ontario, Canada M3B 3K9.

This is a work of fiction. Names, characters, places and incidents are
either the product of the author's imagination or are used fictitiously,
and any resemblance to actual persons, living or dead, business
establishments, events or locales is entirely coincidental.

This edition published by arrangement with Harlequin Books S.A.

® and TM are trademarks of the publisher. Trademarks indicated with
® are registered in the United States Patent and Trademark Office, the
Canadian Trade Marks Office and in other countries.

www.eHarlequin.com

Printed in U.S.A.

ABOUT THE AUTHOR

Imagine a family tree that includes Texas cowboys, Choctaw and Cherokee Indians, a Louisiana pirate and a Scottish rebel who battled side by side with William Wallace. With ancestors like that, it's easy to understand why Texas author and former air force captain Delores Fossen feels as if she was genetically predisposed to writing romances. Along the way to fulfilling her DNA destiny, Delores married an air force top gun who just happens to be of Viking descent. With all those romantic bases covered, she doesn't have to look too far for inspiration.

Books by Delores Fossen

HARLEQUIN INTRIGUE
788—VEILED INTENTIONS
812—SANTA ASSIGNMENT
829—MOMMY UNDER COVER
869—PEEKABOO BABY
895—SECRET SURROGATE
913—UNEXPECTED FATHER
932—THE CRADLE FILES
950—COVERT CONCEPTION
971—TRACE EVIDENCE IN TARRANT COUNTY
990—UNDERCOVER DADDY*

*Five-Alarm Babies

Don't miss any of our special offers. Write to us at the following address for information on our newest releases.

Harlequin Reader Service
U.S.: 3010 Walden Ave., P.O. Box 1325, Buffalo, NY 14269
Canadian: P.O. Box 609, Fort Erie, Ont. L2A 5X3

CAST OF CHARACTERS

Elaina McLemore—When someone tries to kill her, she moves with her adopted son to a small Texas town, changing her name and inventing a missing husband. Then Luke Buchanan shows up, claiming to be her long lost husband—and her baby's father.

Special Agent Luke Buchanan—Robbed of the chance to raise his son when Elaina unknowingly participated in an illegal adoption, nothing will stop him from getting to know his child. But when an elusive criminal comes after them, Luke vows to protect his baby and the only mother his son has ever known.

Christopher—Luke's one-year-old son. He's too young to understand the danger. He only knows that he loves having his daddy around.

George Devereux—Once a successful businessman, now behind bars. Just how far would he go to get back at Luke for arresting him?

Carrie Saunders— Elaina's shop assistant and friend. Carrie has been acting very odd, but she claims she has no idea who's trying to kill Elaina and Luke.

Brenda McQueen—A newcomer to the sleepy Texas town where Elaina's been hiding with Christopher.

Collena Drake—The troubled former cop who now devotes her life to finding illegally adopted babies.

Gary Simpson—Elaina's potentially mentally unstable neighbor. Gary is also jealous of Luke.

Chapter One

Crystal Creek, Texas

"Elaina, your husband is...alive."

The eight-by-ten piece of amber glass that Elaina Allen had been examining slipped from her hand and crashed onto her desk. It didn't break but smashed right into a paper plate containing a half eaten slice of cherry pie. The red sugary filling spattered in every direction.

"Excuse me?" Elaina asked her assistant, Carrie. "What did you say?"

"Your husband is alive," Carrie repeated, nodding frantically. She bobbled up and down on her tiptoes and gave an excited squeal. "He's in Crystal Creek and on the way to the shop. He should be here any minute."

Elaina's heart dropped to her knees.

"There must be some mistake. Daniel's missing in action in the Middle East," Elaina lied. "If he'd been found, the air force would have told me."

Carrie grinned. "Well, they obviously didn't. A snafu maybe, or Daniel probably just wanted to surprise you. Anyway, he stopped by the gas station, and when he got ready to pay, the attendant, Jay, saw your picture in Daniel's wallet. That's when Jay figured out who he was. Jay said after Daniel filled up, he headed in this direction." Carrie's crystal blue eyes widened. "Oh, God. I blew the surprise by telling you, didn't I?"

Elaina couldn't answer. She could only shake her head. No. This couldn't be happening. It just couldn't be.

"Are you all right?" Carrie asked. "You look like you're about to be sick."

There was a reason for that. Elaina knew that the comfortable, safe life she'd created was *over*. Her house and her stained-glass shop were as good as gone. She'd have to go on the run again.

"You're happy about this, right?" Carrie asked. "I mean, this is what you wanted—for Daniel to come home to Christopher and you. You're always saying how much you miss him."

She stared at her shop assistant. They were more than employer and employee. The eternally optimistic Carrie had become her friend. Well, as much of a friend as Elaina could have considering she'd lied to Carrie from day one.

Elaina wasn't immune to the guilt she felt about that, either. She'd never quite come to terms with the pretense.

But she had a more pressing problem.

Daniel Allen was on the way to her shop.

Because that took her to the brink of panic, Elaina almost came clean about everything to Carrie. She almost explained all the lies. And, sweet heaven, there was a mound of lies. But she stopped her near confession and tried to make some sense of all of this.

"Jay said this man had my picture in his wallet?" Elaina clarified, praying for an out.

There had to be an out.

Carrie nodded, and the concern deepened in her eyes. "But he didn't just have your picture. When Jay asked, he told him that he was Daniel Allen."

Then, he was lying. No doubt about it.

Because there was *no* Daniel Allen.

He was the biggest lie of all.

Daniel Allen was an idea that Elaina had concocted to explain why she'd moved to the sleepy Texas town of Crystal Creek. An MIA husband. A grieving heart. The desire to start a new life while keeping hope that her *husband* might be alive and that he might return someday.

Elaine had purposely kept the personal details sketchy, because details could be examined too closely. So, she'd had no picture of her fake husband in case someone compared his looks to her son's. Instead, she'd told everyone that all her photos had been destroyed in a house fire.

The façade had kept some nosey questions from being asked, had given her space and privacy and it had allowed her and her baby, Christopher, to be accepted in a town where newcomers were often treated as outsiders.

That acceptance wouldn't continue once the townsfolk had learned that she was a liar. And this man, this imposter claiming to be Daniel Allen, would expose her.

But why?

Better yet—who was this imposter, and what the heck did he want?

Unfortunately, an answer immediately came to mind. A really bad answer. He might be linked to her late fiancé—the slimy, cheating con man who'd nearly gotten Christopher and Elaina killed.

"Well, don't just sit there," Carrie insisted. She latched on to Elaina's arm to lift her from the chair. "You haven't seen Daniel in over a year. Comb your hair. Put on some makeup. You have to do *something* to get ready for him."

The full impact of that hit her like a heavyweight's fist. Elaina got to her feet somehow. She had to do *something* all right.

She had to get out of there.

Fast.

She'd have to pick up Christopher from the sitter and drive out of town. There probably wouldn't be time to pack or stop for cash. She'd literally have to leave everything behind.

However, before she could even shake off Carrie's grip, Elaina heard the cheerful jingle of the brass and crystal bells that she'd installed over the front door of her shop. It caused her pulse to pound out of control.

Because it no doubt signaled her fake husband's arrival.

This was her own personal version of judgment day.

"Since you don't seem too steady on your feet, I'll bring him in here," Carrie volunteered.

"No!" Elaina caught on to her as she turned to leave.

What remained of Carrie's gleeful expression melted away. "What's wrong?"

"Nothing," Elaina assured her. Yet another lie. "I just need a minute to compose myself. I thought he was dead." Elaina didn't have to fake an overwhelmed expression. She was sure it was there all over her overwhelmed face.

"I'll be right there," Carrie called out to their *visitor.* It was something she would have done for any ordinary customer, but this time there was excitement and anticipation in her voice.

Elaina nodded her thanks for the brief reprieve, and she went to the door that separated her office from the stained-glass shop. With Carrie right behind her, she opened the door just a fraction and peeked out.

His back was to her, and he appeared to be examining a Victorian window panel that Elaina had restored just days earlier.

Whoever he was, he was tall. Six-three at least. Not lanky, either. Solid and formidable. He wore jeans and a brown leather bomber jacket that was nearly the same color as his short, efficiently cut hair.

He turned to the side, and Elaina got a good look of him in profile. That good look was more than enough for her to realize that he was a complete stranger. If he was somehow connected to her late fiancé, Kevin, then she'd never seen him before.

That didn't mean she was safe.

She still had to leave with Christopher and find a new hiding place. Because if this man had found her, *they* could find her.

Elaina blinked back the hot tears that instantly sprang into her eyes, and she silently cursed. Kevin had been dead for over a year, and he was still casting shadows over her life.

"Well?" Carrie prompted in an anxious whisper when Elaina shut the door. "Daniel's here. Aren't you going to run out there, jump into his arms and haul him off to bed?"

Not a chance. The only thing Elaina planned to do was avoid him. "I need you to do me a favor, Carrie. Stall him."

Carrie shook her head. "W-hat? This is the extremely hot husband that you haven't seen in months and months, and you want me to stall him?"

Good point. The next lie came easily. "I need some time to make myself look presentable. I don't want him to see me with pie filling all over me and without a stitch of makeup. I'll only be a minute."

Carrie nodded, eventually, but judging from her bunched up forehead, she didn't understand.

How could she?

And better yet, how would Christopher?

Her son was barely three months past his first birthday. He wouldn't know why his mommy was dragging him away from the only home, bed and toys he'd ever known. One day, she'd have to tell him the truth.

If she remembered the truth by then.

Elaina had lived with the lies for so long that she had to wonder what exactly the truth was. Unfortunately, she might never know.

"Don't keep Daniel waiting too long," Carrie insisted. "And by the way—*he* is hot, just like I figured he'd be." She gave Elaina a wink and then headed back into the shop.

Elaina didn't waste a second. She locked the door behind Carrie and grabbed her purse from beneath her desk. She also took the picture of her son from the top of the filing cabinet. It was her favorite, taken on his first birthday. She stuffed it in her purse, and while she fumbled around the bottom of the shoulder bag for her car keys, she headed to the back exit that led directly to the parking lot.

She estimated that it would take her ten minutes to get to Christopher. She'd call on the way to tell Theresa, the sitter, that Christopher had an appointment with the pediatrician in nearby Luling. An appointment that had slipped her mind until the last minute. Though it would be a first for her to forget something like that, she hoped it'd be a believable lie. She didn't have time for questions.

Elaina located her keys and threw open the exit door. She heard someone trying to get into her office. Carrie maybe. Or maybe the imposter. Elaina ignored the frantic knocks and raced out of the shop.

The winter air was a little more brisk than she'd figured, and a chilly gust temporarily robbed her of her breath. Goose bumps rifled over her arms. The cotton shirt she wore wasn't much of a barrier. It didn't stop her. She ducked her head against the wind and made a beeline toward her car.

"Going somewhere?" she heard someone ask.

It was a man's voice.

Oh, mercy.

His voice, no doubt.

She didn't freeze, though she had to fight her instincts to prevent that from happening. Instead, Elaina began to run toward her car. Even though her heart was pounding and her shoes were slapping on the concrete, she could still hear his footsteps behind her.

Elaina made it all the way to her car before she felt the beefy hand clamp around her arm. She struggled against the grip and slammed her purse into the man's chest.

It didn't help.

As if she weighed nothing, he caught on to her, whirled her around to face him, and he pinned her against the hood of her car.

She screamed. Or rather tried to do that, but he pressed his hand over her mouth.

No profile view of him this time. She caught the full brunt of those lethal looking granite-gray eyes. In fact, lethal described every part of him from his hard body to the expression on his face.

Because he used his body to restrain her, she had no trouble determining that he was strong. No extra body fat on this guy. She also had no trouble spotting the shoulder holster and gun that was only partially concealed beneath his leather jacket.

Still, it didn't matter that she was outsized, out-maneuvered and outgunned. She wouldn't give up without a fight. Especially since this man might go after Christopher. Thankfully, the Crystal Creek police station was just up the block from the shop. She'd yell for help and deal with the inevitable questions later.

First though, she had to get free.

She managed to grab on to his wrist, and she ripped his grip from her mouth. "What do you want?" she snarled.

"Elaina Allen, I presume?" He didn't wait for her to confirm or deny it. "Let me introduce myself. I'm your long-lost husband, Captain Daniel Allen."

Oh, there was some cockiness in that voice tinged with a hint of a Texas drawl, but there were also questions. And accusations.

She forced herself to meet him eye to eye. "You're lying, and you know it."

"Yeah. I guess I do know it. But the way I see it, both of us have told some big fish stories, and both of us have some explaining to do. You start first."

Elaina was about to tell him that she owed him no such explanation and that he'd better let go of her at once or she'd scream, but then she heard Carrie. She peered over the man's shoulder and spotted Carrie in the doorway of the exit.

Elaina cursed under her breath.

So did the man.

She met his gaze to try to figure out what he was about to do. It was entirely possible he might try to kill Carrie so there wouldn't be any witnesses to Elaina's own murder. If that's what he had planned.

Elaina didn't have to wait long to find out.

Much to her shock, the imposter lowered his head and kissed her.

Chapter Two

Luke Buchanan had to keep reminding himself that the woman he was kissing was a liar. Maybe even worse. But just the fact he had to remind himself of that riled him to the core.

Why?

Because he didn't need a reminder that she tasted almost as good as she looked. And she *did* look good, far better than she had from the other end of long range surveillance equipment.

"Play along," Luke warned her, pulling back only slightly.

His warning earned him a nasty little glare. Those ice-blue eyes tapered to slits, and he could have sworn she hissed at him. But maybe that was the brutal November wind that was assaulting them.

"Oh, good," the skinny blond sales clerk said from behind them. "You found each other."

Luke didn't look back at her. He kept his gaze staked to the liar he'd just kissed.

The liar who tasted remarkably like cherry pie.

"Who are you?" the liar demanded.

"Your husband," he lied back. "Trust me, you'll want to go along with that for now. It's in your best interest."

Since his body was still against hers, he felt her go board stiff. She no doubt would have questioned him, or slugged him so she could escape, if the sales clerk hadn't stopped right next to them.

"This is so exciting," the clerk declared. She walked closer and grinned from ear to ear. "I'm a sucker for happy endings."

Well, this wasn't one of them.

Luke knew the clerk was Carrie Saunders. Age twenty-four. Born and raised in Crystal Creek. He was reasonably sure that Ms. Saunders didn't have a clue that she was working for a woman who'd fabricated an entire life. So, in a sense Carrie Saunders was a nonplayer. Or at least she would be once Luke got away from her. He definitely didn't want her or the local police to get suspicious, and he needed to get his *wife* alone so they could have a little chat.

"You wouldn't mind if Elaina left for the day, would you?" Luke asked the other woman. He kept his tone playful and needy, as if he truly were the long-lost husband who'd returned to his loving family.

"Take as much time as you want," Carrie insisted. She wagged her finger at Elaina. "I don't want to see you anywhere near this shop for at least a week. Oh, and if you need someone to babysit Christopher, just give me a call."

Luke assured her that they would, and he slid his arm around Elaina's waist to get her moving. She had that deer-caught-in-the-headlights look, and for a second, he wondered if she was going to try to run away.

"Don't even think about it," Luke mumbled. "You're leaving with me."

He took her keys from her trembling hand and practically pushed her inside her economy-size car. To keep the loving couple façade intact, he pressed a kiss on Elaina's gaping cherry-scented mouth, gave a friendly wave to Carrie and then drove away.

But he didn't breathe any easier now that the first part of his plan had worked. Because there were a lot of steps to this particular plan, and there were pitfalls with every one of them.

"Who are you and what do you want?" she demanded the second they were out of the parking lot.

Since this would no doubt be the beginning of many questions, Luke decided to give her the ground rules. "Here's how things are going to work. I'll ask the questions, and you'll provide the *truthful* answers. We'll start with why you're living this lie."

Her chin came up. "That's none of your business."

"I beg to differ."

It wasn't just his business.

It was his *life*.

"Why the lies?" he pressed.

She stayed a quiet a moment though she continued to stare at him. What she didn't do was answer him. "Are you here because of Kevin?"

Luke figured that name would come up soon enough. "Kevin Arneson, your late fiancé. I never met the man. And that's the only information you're going to get until you start talking. Oh, and remember that part about being truthful. I figure that'll be difficult for you, so try very hard."

No more deer-in-the-headlight look. She aimed her index finger at him. "Let's get something straight. I knew nothing about Kevin's illegal activities. *Nothing.* And I've already paid enough for his stupidity and deception."

"I'll be the judge of that."

She frowned and angled her body back slightly. "What's that supposed to mean?"

"That's another question and still no answer to mine. You're not good at following the rules, so let me clarify the information you're going to tell me. Why all the lies? And why are you in hiding?"

"I have my reasons, and you probably know what they are as well I do." She paused only long enough to draw breath. "I covered my tracks. I haven't used any of the money from Kevin's and my bank accounts or investments. And I haven't contacted a single person that I knew in my former life. So, how in the name of heaven did you find me?"

Luke huffed. Yet another question. This was turning into an annoying interrogation, and his intimidating scowl wasn't working.

Odd.

It usually did.

"Okay. A modification of the rules. Tit for tat, we'll call it. I'll give you a little info, and you'll do the same. I found you through your glass," he informed her.

That gave a moment of hesitation. "You what?"

"When I realized I was looking for Laina McLemore and that you'd disappeared, I started digging for clues. You were a successful stained-glass artist when you lived in San Antonio. I figured that's the line of work you'd fall back on, so I studied your designs, and I started scouring shops and Internet sites until I finally found pieces that I could attribute to your artistic style. People always leave trails when they try to hide." He glanced at her. "Your turn. Start answering my questions."

"Oh, God." But she didn't just say it once. She strung them together and plowed her hands through the sides of her short, spiky, honey-brown hair. "Is that why you're here? Are you one of those men, or did they send you?"

Luke had already geared up to remind her that it was her turn to provide information, but that stopped him cold. "What men?"

"The ones who followed me after Kevin was murdered." Anger fired through her eyes. "Well, if you're one of them, you've wasted your time."

Luke ignored her outburst. "Back up—who are these *men?*"

"They didn't exactly introduce themselves to me, but they did try to run me off the road." Her voice was clipped with anger, and the words came at him like bullets. "There were two of them. Both probably in their early thirties. One had very pale blond hair, and the other had a deep scar on the left side of his face. He wore an eye patch."

Luke wasn't sure what to make of that. Just retelling the event seemed to shake her, but then, this was a woman who was very good at telling believable lies. Still…

"What did these guys want?" he asked.

"I don't know. But I think it had something to do with some computer software that Kevin was modifying for someone he only ever referred to as T. Maybe those men were associated with this T, or maybe they thought I had the modifications or Kevin's research notes. I didn't." She snagged his gaze. "I really don't know anything about my late fiancé's criminal activity, okay? But I've paid for it. I've paid dearly by losing my home, my friends and by having to recreate a life among strangers."

Luke wasn't unaffected by the weariness and pain he heard in her voice, but he pushed aside any sympathy he was feeling by reminding himself of what this woman had done.

She'd robbed him of his life.

"What about the illegal adoption?" he asked. Not easily. It was almost impossible to keep the emotion out of it. "Have you paid for that, too?"

She blinked and pulled in her breath. "How did you know about the adoption?"

"I know a lot about you, Laina Marie McLemore. You're twenty-eight. Born in Bulverde, Texas. A rancher's daughter, though both your parents are dead. I can tell you the name of your third-grade teacher and what you had for dinner last night. What I'm trying to figure out if you were the mastermind behind Arneson's illegal ventures, or were you just along for the very lucrative ride?"

"I knew nothing about Kevin's business dealings or the legality of the adoption." And she was adamant about it, too.

Luke continued to push. "But you went along with it?"

"*Unknowingly* went along with it," she corrected.

When she didn't say more, he made a circular motion with his hand for her to continue.

She started with a huff. "Kevin was sterile, we wanted a baby, and he didn't want me to use donor sperm to get pregnant. He's the one who arranged for the adoption through an attorney in San Antonio. I didn't know it was illegal, not until months after Kevin was murdered, when I read about the illegal adoption ring in the paper. Even then, I didn't know that's how Kevin had gotten Christopher."

"But you suspected it," he accused her.

"No, I didn't. Not until I saw the name of the attorney who'd been arrested. By then, it was too late. I was already in hiding. I'd already established a life here in Crystal Creek. And I knew if I didn't stay hidden, those men would come after me—"

"Ah, the men again," he mocked. "They're getting a lot of playtime in this fantasy world of yours. And it's because of *these men* that you fled San Antonio and went into hiding."

"Yes." She paused. "You don't believe me?"

"No, but that's not important. The important thing is that after a year of digging, I found you."

"Lucky me," she grumbled. She turned in the seat so she was facing him. Her loose, well-worn jeans and dark red cotton shirt whispered against the vinyl seat. Her breath whispered, too. There was more weariness in it, but Luke could see her fighting it off. "Now, it's your turn to answer some questions. Who are you and what do you want?"

"I'm Luke Buchanan." Since the truth would no doubt speed this along, he added, "I'm a federal agent with the Department of Justice."

She put her hand over her heart as if to steady it. "Prove it."

The crisp demand had him doing a double take. For a weary lying woman, she certainly had a lot of resolve left. "Prove what?"

"Show me a badge or some kind of ID."

Jeez. Why couldn't she just confess all?

Irked, Luke reached into his jacket pocket and pulled out his badge. She took it, stared it and even scraped her thumbnail over the picture. Not just once. But twice.

"It's real," he assured her.

She must have agreed because she thrust it back at him. What he wouldn't tell her, yet, was that while the badge was real, this wasn't official Justice Department business.

No.

This was as personal as personal could get.

"I suppose you're here to arrest me for the illegal adoption?" she asked.

"That all depends."

"On what?" Finally, there was slip in her resolve. Her voice cracked.

"You." He came to stop in front of the house, turned off the engine and stared at her.

Probably because she hadn't taken her eyes off him, she hadn't realized where he'd taken her. She glanced out the window for a second before she snapped her head back in his direction. "This is my babysitter's house. What are we doing here?"

He turned toward her so he could see every nuance of her reaction. "Why do you think I'm here?"

"Oh, no." She began to shake her head. "I can't let you do this. You can't arrest me. You don't understand—he's my son. I've raised him since he was three days old. I'm the only mother he's ever known."

"Believe me, I know that."

And that was the only reason he hadn't had Laina McLemore arrested.

"I won't let you take him from me," she insisted.

"You have no choice." And he was just as adamant.

"But you do." Her bottom lip began to tremble,

and she gripped the sides of his leather jacket. "You can walk away from this. You can pretend you never found me."

Luke had thought he would be immune to a reaction like that, but he wasn't. "I can't do that."

The grip she had on his jacket melted away, and she touched her fingers to her mouth. Tears sprang to her eyes. "Oh, God. The birth parents know about Christopher, and they want him back."

"His birth mother is dead." Luke had to take a deep breath after saying that. And another deep breath before he could continue. "But his birth father does indeed want him back."

Twin tears spilled down her cheeks. "Then, I need to talk to him. I need to make him understand how much Christopher means to me."

"You're already talking to him, and there's nothing you can say or do to make me change my mind. Christopher is *my* son."

Chapter Three

Elaina's breath vanished. And her heart. God, her heart. It was pounding so fast and hard that she thought her ribs might crack.

This was her nightmare come true. Well, one of them anyway. The only thing worse than this would be another attack from those men. But this was an attack of a different kind.

Luke Buchanan was Christopher's birth father.

Or was he?

On the surface it seemed stupid to challenge him, but she was desperate. "Why should I believe you?" she asked. "Show me some proof that he's your son."

She figured that might buy her some time. It didn't. As if he'd anticipated the question, he calmly reached inside his leather jacket and produced a manila envelope. Elaina also noticed the gun tucked in a leather shoulder holster. It looked as authentic and official as his badge. Luke Buchanan seemed to be the real deal.

"Let me start with how I found out that you had my son. A woman named Collena Drake, a former cop, has been digging through the hundreds of files left by the criminals who orchestrated the adoptions, among other things. She got in touch with me and was able to tell me the names of the couple who'd illegally adopted Christopher."

"Collena Drake could have been wrong," Elaina offered. "And the records could have been wrong, too. After all, the people who put them together were criminals. You just said so yourself."

He ignored her, opened the envelope and extracted a picture. "That's Taylor, my late wife."

Elaina took the photo from him, dreading what she might see. It was the picture of a couple on their wedding day. The bride, dressed in white, was a beautiful brunette. The groom, Luke Buchanan, wore a tux.

"That's still not proof," Elaina insisted.

Luke Buchanan's calm demeanor remained in place. From the envelope, he produced a marriage license. He placed it on the seat between them. Elaina was about to repeat her doubt, but the next document kept her quiet.

It was a lab slip indicating a positive pregnancy test.

The date on the slip was eight months prior to Christopher's birth.

"In addition to the lab results, this is a report that details how I learned about what happened to Taylor and our baby." He plopped the stapled pages onto the stack. "There's an eyewitness account of Taylor arriving at the Brighton Birthing Center just outside San Antonio. She was in labor. The eyewitness helped her into the E.R. section of the building and then left. All of this happened August eleventh of last year."

That information hit her hard. Because August eleventh was Christopher's birthday. And his place of birth was indeed the Brighton Birthing Center. Still, Elaina wasn't going to accept this blindly.

"Eyewitness accounts can be falsified," she countered.

"Not this one. It came from the cab driver who took Taylor from our house to the birthing center. He has absolutely no reason to lie."

She swallowed hard. "Maybe not, but that still doesn't prove Christopher is your son. There were probably dozens of babies born that day."

"Three." He paused a heartbeat and snagged her gaze. "But only one boy. Seven pounds, four ounces. Twenty-one inches long. Sound familiar?"

Oh, mercy. It did.

Elaina felt the tears burn hot in her eyes, and she didn't even try to fight them back.

"Take a good look at that photo," he said, fishing out the wedding picture from the pile. "You'll see that Taylor and I are Christopher's birth parents."

Though it was nearly impossible to see clearly through the thick tears, Elaina did study the photo he handed her. Luke and Taylor Buchanan were both brunettes. As was Christopher. And though she hadn't made the connection when she first met Agent Buchanan, she could see it now.

Christopher had his eyes.

Except on her son, the color seemed softer. Kinder. Rainy-cloud-gray, she'd whimsically called them. It was ironic to see those same eyes on this man who could destroy her.

And there was no doubt about it—losing Christopher *would* destroy her.

That's why Elaina didn't give up. She couldn't. He'd made a good case, but other than the similar eyes, he certainly hadn't proven anything.

"Why did your wife have to take a taxi to the Brighton Birthing Center?" she asked. "Where were you during all of this?"

"I was on a deep-cover assignment trying to stop a terrorist attack." A muscle flickered in his jaw. "Taylor and I were having problems, and we'd gotten a legal separation right before I left. I didn't know she was pregnant until after I returned. Then, I learned she'd died of complications from a C-section. I also learned that the baby, our son, had been adopted, but the records had supposedly been destroyed. The records didn't surface until the police busted the illegal operation and Collena Drake decided to devote all her time to locating the missing kids. That's why it took me this long to find you."

Each word added dead weight to her heart. Because this was unfortunately all starting to make sense.

"I found you eight days ago," he continued. The

calm façade seemed to slip a little. There was a touch of hot, raw emotion in his voice. "And I put you under surveillance."

She shook her head. "I didn't know."

"Of course, you didn't. I do a lot of surveillance in my job, and I'm very good at it."

No doubt. It riled her that someone had been able to intrude into her life without her even realizing it. That gave her the resolve she'd been searching for. "So, you watched me and decided to step into my fake life and pretend you're my husband?"

He nodded. "You made it easy for me to do that. I had a fellow agent ask around town. He pretended to be interested in having some church windows repaired. And he learned there were no photos of your fake spouse. No specific physical accounts or descriptions. No one around here seemed to know what Daniel Allen looks like."

"I didn't want anyone comparing the photo to Christopher. Since he doesn't look like me, I just told people that he took after his father." Elaina paused and tried to fight off the dark reality she felt closing in around her. "And maybe he does."

"*Maybe?* You still have doubts after everything I've shown you?"

"I have to have doubts." She slapped her hand on the documents he'd shown her. "Doubts are the only thing that prevents me from screaming and running inside to hide my son from you. Besides, you have no DNA proof—"

"I do have proof. I got back the results about two hours ago. That's why I'm here."

There was no way Elaina could have braced herself for the final paper that he took from the envelope. She shook her head when he tried to hand it to her, but he finally dropped it onto her lap.

She had no choice. Even though she didn't want to look at it, her eyes refused to cooperate. It was indeed a DNA test, and it identified Luke Buchanan as the father of one Christopher Allen.

That put another fracture in her heart.

"This can't be accurate," she challenged. "You don't have Christopher's DNA so you had nothing to make the comparison."

But his expression said differently. "After I found you, I took a pacifier that Christopher had left in his car seat. And before you accuse me of breaking and entering, I didn't. I had a warrant."

She hadn't thought it possible, but her heart pounded even faster. Elaina frantically searched for holes in his case and found one. "If you have this proof," she said picking up the DNA test, "then, why pretend to be my long-lost husband?"

"Because there's something I need from you."

He let that hang between them for several moments before he scooped up all the papers and put them back into the envelope. "Here's what's going to happen—we'll go inside and you'll make introductions. To the sitter and especially to my son. For the next few days, I'll pretend to be the husband that you've so cleverly created."

But once they were inside, he could take Christopher. "And if I don't agree?"

He lifted his shoulder and slipped the envelope back into his jacket. "Then, I call the FBI, and have you arrested for participating in an illegal adoption. Then, I take Christopher from Crystal Creek, and you'll never see him again."

Mercy, he was indeed holding all the cards. "And if I cooperate?" She held her breath, praying for some good news in all of this.

"I'll still take Christopher, eventually. After he's gotten to know me." More of that calm reserve slipped away. He scrubbed his hand over his face. "Look, I know you've been a good mother to my son, but he's mine, and I have no intentions of giving him up. We might even be able to work out visitation rights for you—if you can ever convince me that you didn't do anything illegal to get him."

Elaina was about to ask how she could ever prove that, but she caught some movement out of the corner of her eye. She looked out the window. Theresa, the sitter, was making her way across the yard toward the car.

Elaina groaned. She didn't need this visit. Not now. She still somehow had to convince Luke Buchanan to leave and never come back.

A smiling Theresa tapped on the window, and Elaina reluctantly lowered it. The elderly woman had sugar-white hair and smelled of ginger cookies. Christopher's favorite. Theresa had no doubt been baking them for him.

Theresa's attention went straight to Luke Buchanan. "Daniel, it's so good to meet you," Theresa said before Elaina could offer any explanation. "I'm Theresa Gafford. I babysit your precious son."

Luke nodded and even flashed a smile. The facial gesture seemed stiff as if it'd been a while since he'd done that. "Good to meet you, too, Theresa."

There were tears in Theresa's eyes and a smile on her face. "Thank goodness you're home. You're the answer to so many prayers."

More like the answer to a nightmare. "Carrie called you to tell you that Daniel was here," Elaina said to Theresa.

"Yes. And Jay from the gas station, too," Theresa verified. "It's impossible to keep secrets around here."

It was a comment that caused Elaina to cough.

Theresa motioned toward the house. "Christopher's taking a nap, but I can wake him. I suspect you're anxious to see him." She smiled. "Or maybe you two should just head home and I can bring him after he's awake."

"No." Elaina quickly vetoed that. She wanted to spend no more time alone with this man. Of course, she didn't want him around Christopher, either. "We'll come back later."

Much later.

"Darling," Luke said. The term of endearment

seemed as foreign as his smile. "If you don't mind, I'd love to see my son. Now."

Those stormy eyes warned her to defy him.

Elaina cast him her own warning, but she knew his carried far more weight. He could have her arrested. He could legally remove Christopher from her life.

Because she had no choice, Elaina reached for the door handle. She would cooperate, for now. But there was no way she could let him take Christopher.

Luke got out of the car at the same time she did, and he quickly went to her and slid his arm around her waist. Since Theresa was ahead of them and couldn't see, Elaina tossed him a scowl and pushed her elbow against his ribs to keep some distance between them.

"Daniel, the three of you will have to come for dinner once you're settled," Theresa said.

"Thank you," Luke answered. "I'd like that."

Elaina mumbled the same fake gratitude under her breath, knowing that there'd be no dinner. If she couldn't talk Luke into leaving, she'd have to consult an attorney about what her rights were.

If she even had rights.

It was entirely possible that she didn't.

"Oh, I nearly forgot," Theresa said, stopping on the top porch step. The wind rifled through her hair when she turned around to face Elaina. "About two hours ago I went over to your house to get Christopher his bunny. You forgot to bring it this morning.

Anyway, while I was there, two men drove up in a black car and asked to speak to you."

Elaina stopped, too, and stared up at the woman. "Who were they?"

"Census takers, they said." Theresa's forehead bunched up. "I thought it was a little early for that, but they said they needed to ask you some questions. I told them you might be at your shop and let them know that it was easy to find since it was on Main Street just up from the police station."

Elaina was more than a little concerned. In the entire year she'd been in Crystal Creek, no one had come looking for her. It seemed too much of a coincidence that she'd have three visitors in the same day.

"Did these men show you any ID?" Luke wanted to know.

Theresa shook her head. "No. I didn't ask for it. Oh, dear. Should I have?"

"No," he assured her. "It's just they might have been from the air force, to give Elaina official notification that I was coming home."

"They definitely said they were census takers." Theresa paused. "But to be honest with you, they made me a little uncomfortable. Especially the one with the eye patch."

"Eye patch?" Elaina repeated, her voice barely making a sound.

Theresa nodded. "You just don't see many eye patches these days, and this guy had a scar to go with it. Anyway, he didn't talk much, but the tall blond man with him said they'd come back later to discuss things with you."

Elaina looked at Luke, and would have given him an I-told-you-so glare if she hadn't been so terrified.

Luke reacted. And his reaction terrified her even more.

He shoved his hand inside his jacket so he could grip his weapon, and his gaze fired around them.

"Get inside," he ordered. "*Now.*"

Chapter Four

"What's wrong?" Theresa, asked. "What's happening?"

Luke didn't answer her. Instead, he hooked his arms around both women, hurried them inside and locked the door. He did a quick visual scan of the interior of the place. It was clean and homey with the smell of freshly made cookies. But the main thing he wanted to establish was that there were no gunmen inside.

There weren't any signs of them. Hopefully, it would stay that way.

"Are the other doors locked?" he asked Theresa.

Her eyes widened. "Yes. I did that before I drove over to Elaina's. I haven't been out back since then, so I'm sure they're still locked."

Good. A locked door wouldn't stop pros, but it might slow them down. "Check, just to make sure."

Theresa didn't question him. She hurried to do what he'd asked.

Luke automatically went through a mental checklist. According to the sitter, the baby was asleep. The men were likely only minutes away. Maybe less. And basically, once he'd verified that the doors were locked, Theresa's house was about as secure as he was going to be able to make it without equipment and assistance.

"I can't believe this is happening," Elaina mumbled. She rubbed her hands up and down her arms and paced.

Yeah. Luke was having a hard time believing it, as well. "You're sure these guys are a real threat?"

She stopped in midpace. "Oh, they're real. I'm just wondering why they didn't go to the shop after Theresa told them that's where I was."

Probably because the shop was so close to the police station. If the men were up to no good, that's the last place they'd want to confront Elaina. More likely scenarios were that they'd either hang around her house. Or they'd come here.

"Everything's locked up," Theresa said, returning to the room.

Luke took out his gun and pulled back a lacy white curtain so he could see outside.

"Please tell me what's wrong." Theresa said. She sounded on the verge of tears.

Elaina answered before he could. "There are war protestors who might have followed Daniel to Crystal Creek. You know how some people are opposed to the military being overseas. Daniel just doesn't want to take any chances that these protestors might be fanatics."

Luke wasn't surprised that Elaina's lie had come so easily, but this time, he was thankful for it. He needed to focus on what had to be done. Because, simply put, his son could be in danger.

"Go to Christopher," he instructed Theresa. "If the windows aren't locked, then lock them. Close the curtains, turn off any lights and stay with him until we're certain these *protestors* are gone."

Theresa nodded. "Should I call the sheriff?"

Luke didn't really want to have to deal with the locals on this. Not until he was certain what he was dealing with. "No. Don't call him yet. This might turn out to be nothing."

The sitter rushed away again, headed toward one of the side rooms of the house, and Luke turned his attention to the street. Would the men arrive in a car, as they'd apparently done at Elaina's, or were they on foot? Luke had to be prepared for either.

He took out his cell phone and pressed in the number for his backup: a friend and fellow agent, Rusty Kaplan. He was waiting just a few miles away.

"I need your help," Luke told Rusty. "Look for two men driving around town in a black car. One is blond. The other is wearing an eye patch. If you find them, take them in for questioning."

Rusty assured Luke that he would, and Luke hung up, slipping the phone back into his jacket pocket.

"I blame you for this," Elaina snarled in a hoarse whisper. She frantically looked around the room and extracted an umbrella from a tall reed basket by the door. Presumably, she planned to use it as a weapon.

Luke moved to another window in the living room where he had a better view of the street and the side of the yard. He kept his gun ready.

"How do you figure?" he asked.

"Those men must have followed you to Crystal Creek."

Luke couldn't completely rule it out, but that scenario wasn't very likely. "If someone followed me, I would have noticed."

"Maybe not," she fired back.

"*I would have noticed,*" he insisted.

Maybe someone hadn't followed him per se, but they might have gotten the information from Collena Drake and backtracked until they found Elaina.

Now the question was—what the hell did they want?

Luke didn't want to get into a lengthy discussion, or argument with Elaina to try to figure all of that out. Later, he would have to learn what kind of hornet's nest her dead fiancé had left her to deal with. Because according to what Elaina had said, these men were almost certainly connected to Kevin.

Unless…

There was an outside shot that they were connected to him. Oh, man. He hoped that wasn't the case.

Elaina moved to the window next to him and stared out. "Do you see them?"

"No." In fact, no one seemed to be around.

Except Elaina, of course.

She moved so close to him that he caught her scent. Something fresh, floral and feminine. Something that he didn't want to smell or notice. Luke stepped away from her and moved to a window in the adjoining dining room.

Of course, she and her feminine scent quickly followed him. "How long before you hear something from your partner?"

"Soon. He'll be as thorough and as fast as he can possibly be." Luke only hoped that it wouldn't be hard to spot two strangers in the small town. Thankfully, there wouldn't be many guys with an eye patch.

"This is a nightmare," she mumbled. "And this is what I've been trying to avoid for over a year."

Luke spared her a glance to see how she was physically reacting to the situation. Elaina had a white-knuckled grip on the perky yellow umbrella, but other than that, she seemed to be holding up.

"You sure that's all you were trying to avoid?" he asked.

Elaina's grip tightened even more. "What's that supposed to mean?"

"Maybe you were trying to avoid me because I'm Christopher's father."

She probably would have pounced on that accusation if Luke hadn't noticed the car driving toward the house. He held up his left hand to cut off anything she might have said, and then raced back to the front door so he'd have a direct shot if it became necessary.

Luke waited, his heart in his throat, as the black

four-door car slowly approached and stopped in front of the house. A blond man was driving. The guy with the eye patch was riding shotgun.

This didn't look good.

He took out his phone and called Rusty Kaplan again. "The suspects are at the sitter's house. Get here ASAP."

He put his phone away so he could focus on keeping his weapon aimed and ready. Beside him, Elaina did the same. She lifted her umbrella.

Luke rolled his eyes at her attempt to defend herself. "Get down on the floor," he ordered.

"I want to protect Christopher," she countered.

"Well, it won't happen with an umbrella. Get on the floor in case they fire shots."

"Oh, God," she mumbled.

She was obviously terrified at the thought of bullets flying.

So was Luke.

But it wouldn't help matters if Elaina got hurt. In fact, it was his responsibility to keep everyone in the house safe. He might not have been the one to bring these men to Crystal Creek, but there was too much at stake for him to not make sure they did no harm— especially to his son.

Instead of getting on the floor, she stooped down next to him and put her shoulder against the door so she could peek out the stained-glass sidelights. "I can't just hide. I have to do something to stop them."

Luke knew how she felt.

"For now, the best way to help is stay put. Backup in on the way."

The men didn't leave their parked car. They just sat there, watching the house, occasionally saying something to each other.

More than anything, Luke wanted to go out there to confront them. But that was too big of a risk. If he got shot or hurt, then that would leave Christopher, Elaina and Theresa without protection. He couldn't do that. But he could try to make sense of all of this while they were waiting.

"If these guys are looking for Kevin's software modifications, what do you think they'll do to you if they can't get them?" he asked.

"They'll kill me." Her voice wasn't shaky or trembling. Nor was she hesitant.

Luke didn't take his eyes off the car or the men inside. "And these guys didn't show up until after you'd adopted Christopher?"

"That's right." Now, there was some hesitation. "Why do you ask?"

"Because they might not be associated with software but with the adoption itself. Maybe they're working for someone who wanted to cover their tracks."

"Maybe. But the people involved with the adoption ring have already been arrested."

"That's why they'd need to hire someone on the outside to do it for them," Luke pointed out.

Especially if their crimes included murder.

There, Luke had finally made a connection that he

didn't want to make. A connection that linked him with these goons in the car. And it also might link them to his estranged wife's suspicious death. "What did this so-called adoption agency tell you about Christopher's birth mother? Specifically, what did they say about her death?"

"Nothing."

"They didn't even tell you that she was dead?"

Elaina's eyes widened, and she shook her head. "I didn't know. The paperwork was sketchy at best, and I never dealt directly with them. Only Kevin spoke to them."

Great. One crook dealing with a bunch of others who were making a fortune in the baby-selling business. The police had estimated that Kevin had paid nearly fifty thousand dollars for his son.

"You think they killed your wife?" Elaina asked.

The woman was certainly good at connecting the dots. "Someone did," Luke mumbled.

He heard Elaina suck in her breath. Luke had a similar mental reaction. Just thinking about Taylor's death affected him that way. Even though Taylor and he had fallen out of love long before their separation, he would always blame himself for not being there to protect her.

"I had Taylor's body exhumed," Luke explained. "They're doing the autopsy in a day or two, but it looks as if she had help dying from complications from a C-section."

That was all Luke had time to say.

Because the two men stepped from the car and started walking toward the house.

ELAINA LIFTED HER umbrella, knowing it was probably futile and borderline stupid, but also knowing that she wouldn't let these men get to her son.

If that's what they intended.

It was entirely possible they'd come just to kill her. She wasn't ready to die, but she preferred that to any attempt they might make to harm Christopher.

The two men stopped at the end of the walk and stared at the house. The blonde said something to the other and then glanced over his shoulder at Elaina's car. They obviously knew she was there.

Would they just try to break in?

Would they storm the place?

Maybe. But with Luke there, she was betting they wouldn't be successful. For the first time since she'd laid eyes on the man who could destroy her, she was thankful Luke was with her. Protecting Christopher was everything now, and though Elaina had plenty of doubts about Luke Buchanan, she didn't doubt his ability to keep her baby safe.

But safe from what?

Were these men connected to Kevin, or as Luke had suggested, were they connected to the adoption? If so, had they already murdered Luke's wife?

That chilled her to the bone. Because if this was linked to the adoption, then they might plan to go after Christopher. Maybe they'd do that to eliminate a connection to a murdered woman. But if that was true, then Luke would be a target, as well.

The men began walking again. Beside her, she was aware that Luke tensed his muscles. But that was only reaction. He aimed his weapon directly at them.

"Move away from the door," Luke whispered. And even though it was a whisper, it was still an order.

This time, Elaina obeyed, because she knew that bullets could easily go through the wood. Theresa's fifty-something-year-old home wasn't designed to block intruders.

Elaina crawled to the side. Not far. She wanted to be near that door if the men tried to break it down.

"There's my backup," she heard Luke say.

Elaina scrambled to the window to see what he meant, and she saw the other car approach. But it didn't just *approach*. The dark blue SUV came screeching around the corner and came to a jerky stop right behind the men's vehicle. And that wasn't all. The agent who got out was armed. He pointed a huge gun right at the men.

"Stay put," Luke warned her.

Luke barreled out the door, probably to give back up to the backup. Elaina didn't mind. She wanted those two men arrested and away from Christopher and her.

She couldn't hear what Luke said fo them, but both men lifted their hands into the air. Luke kept his gun trained on them while Luke's partner, a tall brown-haired man, rushed to handcuff the two men.

The agent also searched them. Both men had not just one weapon but two each.

Luke and the agent didn't waste any time. They ushered the men into the backseat of the agent's SUV. Elaina sat there, her face glued to the sidelight window, and she watched as Luke said something else to them. The men didn't respond. A few moments later, the agent drove away with the men.

Elaina got to her feet, though the adrenaline made her jittery. Later, when all of this sank in, she was certain she'd be furious at those imbeciles for putting her through this.

Luke came through the door, and he tucked his gun back into his shoulder holster. "Agent Kaplan is taking them to the local jail. As soon as they're processed, I'll go there and assist with the interview."

"So, they didn't admit to any guilt when you arrested them?"

He shook his head and blew out a weary breath. "No. But unless they have permits to carry concealed weapons, we can hold them on that for a while."

For a while didn't sound nearly long enough.

"Why would those men have killed your wife?" Elaina asked. She shoved the umbrella back into the basket and made sure that Theresa was still in the nursery. She didn't want the woman overhearing any of this. "You think they did it to get Christopher from her so they could hand him over to the lawyers running the adoption ring?"

Luke adjusted his leather jacket so the weapon wouldn't be visible. "That's one theory."

She snapped toward him. "There's more than one?"

He nodded. Raked his fingers over his eyebrow. "Right before I went on the deep cover-up last year, I arrested a man named George Devereux. He was slime, into too many different crimes to name. Devereux vowed revenge because I arrested him. I haven't been able to prove it, but it's possible that Devereux murdered Taylor shortly after she gave birth. It's also possible that he or one of his henchmen sold or gave Christopher to the adoption ring."

Elaina felt as if someone had punched her in the stomach. It took several seconds to regain her breath and some semblance of composure. It took her slightly longer than that to manage to think his theory through. On the one hand, it would make her feel marginally better to put the blame on Luke. But on the other hand, she didn't want a heavy-duty criminal like Devereux to be involved in this.

"So then, why would Devereux's men come after me?" she demanded to know. "I certainly can't link him to Christopher's adoption or to Taylor's death."

"Maybe Devereux didn't want to stop with Taylor." Luke paused and met her gaze. "Maybe he's had time to stew while sitting in prison and wants to continue his revenge."

"Oh, God." Elaina dropped back a step. "You mean Christopher?"

"Yeah," he confirmed.

Elaina groaned and felt the sickening knot form in her stomach. "So, either George Devereux or Kevin might have spawned this?"

"There's only one way to find out which one. Those two men will provide the answers."

Yes. The men. With all the talk about Devereux and revenge, she'd nearly forgotten that they might be very close to learning what this was really about. In fact, if the men confessed to trying to kill her, then they'd be off the streets for a long, long time. Their confession and incarceration could give her the safety she'd been praying for and the freedom to resume a normal life.

For all the good it'd do her now.

Luke Buchanan's arrival had changed everything, and Elaina didn't think they would agree on what she considered a *normal life*. Heck, he could still try to have her arrested for the illegal adoption.

Elaina felt sick. That feeling didn't go away when she heard Theresa call out. "I hope those protestors are gone. Christopher's up from his nap. Is it okay if I bring him out there?"

She was on the verge of saying no, but the word stuck in her throat. Luke, however, seemed to have no trouble responding. Obviously following the sound of Theresa's voice, he headed straight for Christopher.

Elaina rushed after him. It was like a train wreck about to happen.

Luke paused in the doorway of the nursery, and

since he took up nearly the entire space, Elaina had to stand on her tiptoes to see what had stopped the agent in his tracks.

Christopher was there. He wore the denim overalls and long-sleeved knit blue shirt that she'd dressed him in that morning. He was standing, holding on to the arm of the rocking chair where Theresa was seated.

"The protestors are gone?" Theresa asked.

"They're gone," Luke assured her, but his attention was focused solely Christopher.

Luke stepped toward the baby. Elaina's instincts screamed to stop him. But she couldn't. She could only stand there and watch as Luke reached down and gently lifted her son into his arms.

Chapter Five

Luke forgot to breathe.

In fact, he forgot everything when he picked up his son. He'd never thought anything could feel like this. It was magic. Pure magic. And the weight of the world slipped off Luke's shoulders.

Well, in one way it did.

In another, he knew instantly that he would do whatever it took to protect—and claim—his son.

Christopher whimpered a little and tossed a questioning glance at Elaina before turning those suspicious gray eyes back on Luke. Eyes that were a perfect replica of Luke's own.

The genetics didn't stop there. Luke had seen baby pictures of himself, and Christopher was a little DNA copy, right down to his chocolate-brown hair.

His son's bottom lip quivered, and judging from his expression he was about to cry.

"It's okay," Theresa said, her voice soothing. "It's Da Da. Remember, we talk about Da Da. Well, Da Da's come home to be with you."

Even more skepticism came into Christopher's eyes, but he tested out the syllables he'd heard his sitter say. "Da Da."

Behind him, Luke heard Elaina's breath shatter, and he looked back to see the tears streaming down her cheeks. Theresa was crying, too, but Luke was almost positive that the sitter's tears were of the happy variety.

He couldn't say the same for Elaina.

Those were real tears of pain and anguish. Luke understood them. Though he hadn't cried, he'd felt those same raw emotions from the moment that he learned he had a son. It'd ripped his heart into pieces. Now, just holding his baby, just hearing him say those precious sounds, made all the pain and anguish melt away.

"I'll give the three of you some privacy," Theresa insisted. She stood and left the room, closing the door behind her.

His son smelled like baby powder and cookies. Luke brushed a kiss on Christopher's forehead, and because he suddenly wasn't feeling too steady on his feet, he sat down in the rocker. Elaina sat, as well. Groaning softly, she sank down onto the floor and buried her face in her hands.

That seemed to be Christopher's cue to get moving. The little boy squirmed to get out of his arms, and though Luke hated to let go of him, his son was insistent. Fearing that he might drop him, Luke finally deposited him onto the floor. He held on to him until Christopher plopped into a sitting position and then immediately crawled toward Elaina.

The only mother his son had ever known.

Christopher used her knees to pull himself up to a rather precarious standing position. He slapped at her hands until she lowered them. Despite her tear-stained face, the little boy smiled at her. It wasn't an ordinary smile, either. It was a smile of joy and love.

Seeing that love aimed at Elaina put a fist around Luke's heart. On the one hand, he despised the woman who'd perhaps robbed him of months with his son. On the other hand, she was the center of his baby's world.

For now, anyway.

She reached out and pulled Christopher to her. "You can't take him away from me."

Maybe not right away he couldn't, but if she was innocent Luke couldn't see including her permanently in his life. Except for perhaps visitation rights. He only hoped that was enough.

"Concentrate on the here and now," Luke told her. "I will raise my son, and that'll be a lot easier to do with your *cooperation*."

That sent her gaze slicing to his. "And what do you consider cooperation?"

"Help Christopher through this adjustment."

She huffed. "You're talking about your plan. You want me to pretend to be your loving wife until you're comfortable enough to take Christopher."

"I don't want him to have too many changes at once," Luke clarified. "I want this to be the easiest possible transition for him. If we're in the house that he considers home, if you're there, and if we can create a safe, nurturing environment for him, then—"

"Then you'll wait until he gets to know you and then take him."

Yes. But Luke couldn't say that to her, not with those tears in her eyes. "We'll see what we can work out," he offered.

And under the circumstances, it was the best he could give her.

They sat there, both looking at the little boy they loved and wanted. And there was no doubt about it. Luke did love this child. Unconditional, total love. Even though he'd just met him for the first time, he couldn't imagine a life without his son.

Christopher babbled something indistinguishable and dropped back to the floor so he could crawl to his toys. Luke got down there with him, but before the playtime could start, his cell phone rang.

Hating the interruption but knowing it could be critical, Luke answered the call. "Agent Buchanan."

"It's me, Rusty," he heard his friend say. "We made it to the jail without incident. The sheriff is booking the guys now. This is all just preliminary, but I checked their IDs. Their names are Damien Weathers and Simon Foster. Neither have a permit to carry concealed weapons so we can hold them. I ran their priors. Both also have records for burglary and some outstanding traffic tickets, but that's it."

That didn't mean the two were innocent of this

particular count. Whatever this *count* was. And it didn't mean they weren't the ones who'd tried to hurt Elaina a year ago.

"I'll come down for the interviews," Luke insisted.

"There won't be any, not for a while at least. Both lawyered up, and both are giving us the silent treatment. You're not getting anything out of these guys."

Luke mentally cursed. "When will the lawyer be there?"

"Not until morning. No interviews, no interrogations until then."

He mentally cursed even more. It wasn't what he wanted to hear. But on the upside, as long as the men were behind bars, then Christopher was probably safe. Still, Luke wasn't about to take any chances.

"You take care of things there with your little boy," Rusty insisted. "I'll arrange to install the security equipment we discussed."

Luke had nearly forgotten about that. Not good. He needed to be totally focused because that equipment was a necessity. He wanted it installed in the wooded area behind Elaina's house. With a motion-activated silent alarm, it would warn in advance if someone tried to sneak onto her property.

"I can get one of the agents from the Austin office to install it," Rusty explained. "We'll connect it to your cell phone signal so we won't need to put any equipment inside Elaina's house."

"That'd be a big help," Luke assured him.

"No problem. I'll spend the night here at the

sheriff's office. In the mean time, I'll keep digging and see if I can find any outstanding warrants on them. I'll have their car impounded, as well. Something might turn up that we can use to put these guys away for a long, long time."

"Thanks, Rusty."

Elaina was staring at him when he ended the call. "What happened?"

"The men are in jail. I'll interrogate them tomorrow after their lawyer shows up." But no lawyer was going to stop him from getting answers.

"So, what do we do until then?" she asked.

It would not be an answer she liked, but it was the only answer Luke was going to give her.

"We take Christopher to your house," he said. "*Together.* I'll start getting acquainted with my son."

She swallowed hard. "Does that mean you'll be staying the night?"

It was yet another answer she wouldn't like. Actually, Luke didn't like it much, either. "Of course. That's been my plan all along," he reminded her.

But he'd come up with that plan before he'd ever met Elaina face-to-face. Before he'd had these stupid lustful thoughts about her.

Luke definitely hadn't counted on the attraction.

Now, he had to figure out how to get past it. Because if he didn't, it was going to be a very long night.

SHE COULD RUN AGAIN.

That was the one thought that kept going through

Elaina's mind. She could wait until Luke was asleep and try to sneak out with Christopher. Yes, she'd probably be breaking the law, but she couldn't bear the thought of losing her son.

Elaina unlocked the front door of her house, and as she always did, reset the security system. She motioned for Luke to walk in ahead of her while she aimed a few daggers his way. Not that it would do any good. He obviously wasn't going to change his mind about this asinine plan.

Luke had a sleeping Christopher cradled in his arms. The baby obviously hadn't finished his nap because he'd fallen sound asleep on the short drive from Theresa's to the house. It wasn't unusual for him to do that, but because Christopher wasn't awake, that meant she'd have to spend time *alone* with Luke. Elaina was not looking forward to that.

"His bedroom is at the end of the hall," Elaina explained. She showed Luke the way, but she didn't give him a tour or even a friendly expression. She simply opened the door to the nursery and pointed to the crib.

Luke gently lay the baby down and covered him with a pale blue quilt. What he didn't do was leave. He stayed right there, looking down at Christopher.

Elaina didn't want to speculate about what he was thinking, but she couldn't help herself. Luke was no doubt realizing how much he loved this child. That love would only make him more adamant about taking Christopher.

Unless she did something to stop it.

She had to either sneak away with Christopher, or convince Luke to give up his plan.

"How long will you be staying in my house?" she demanded in a whisper.

He turned, frowned and walked toward her. Elaina automatically backed up to keep some distance between them, but he closed that distance.

Luke leaned in and practically put his mouth right against her ear. "First things first—how good is your security system?" he asked.

She'd anticipated that he might say a lot of things, but that wasn't one of them. Though she should have anticipated it. Because after what'd just happened with those men, it was relevant.

"It's an excellent system," she explained. Elaina whispered, too, and then she inched back away from him. "I had it installed right after I moved here. It's monitored through the sheriff's office and covers all the windows and doors."

"What about the backyard and those thick trees that divide your house from your neighbor's property?"

That'd been her concern when she moved in, as well. The lots were huge, at least an acre each, so there was plenty of space in between the individual homes. "There are motion-activated lights that come on in the front and back porches if someone approaches at night."

He nodded, and it seemed to be an approval. "Make sure the system is on at all times. A fellow agent will be adding some extra equipment in the wooded area. If someone trips the system, I'll be alerted through my cell phone."

That hiked up her blood pressure. "You think those men are going to get out of jail tomorrow?"

He whispered again and closed the already narrow space between them. "Not if I can help it. I just need you to be cautious."

For some reason, that riled her. Maybe it was the comment. Or maybe it was the closeness. Elaina definitely didn't like being close to Luke. It was too much of a reminder that he was a man.

A man that she was stupidly attracted to.

"Oh, I'm cautious all right," Elaina insisted. "Remember, I didn't move to Crystal Creek for the beautiful scenery. I moved here because those two men tried to run me off the road."

Their gazes met and held.

For way too long.

Something happened. The air changed, maybe. The curl of heat returned. Her body seemed to suggest things that it should never have suggested. She warned her body to knock it off because it wasn't going to get Luke Buchanan.

Elaina folded her arms over her chest and looked away. "How long will you be here?" she repeated. Best to get her mind back on business.

He glanced back at the crib. "Originally, I'd planned a week or two."

After the reaction she'd just had to him, that sounded like a lifetime. "And now?"

"It'll depend on what happens with that interrogation tomorrow. I want to get to know my son, but first, I have to make sure he's safe."

"Trust me, that's my priority, too. What I don't get is why we have to pretend to be a couple."

He moved closer still, and some frustration crept into his whisper. "I've already told you that I want Christopher to get to know me here, in the place he considers home. I'd rather do that without a lot of questions from your friends and neighbors. Besides, it's only a temporary arrangement. I'll be out of your life soon enough."

That improved her posture. "I don't want you out of my life, not if that means that you take Christopher with you."

Another glance at the crib, and he caught her arm to move her in the hall. She welcomed it. No more whispered, cheek-to-cheek conversations.

"I'm trying to be fair about this," he said, huffing. "Why don't we call a truce? Just let me get to know my son. Let me take care of these possible security issues. And in a few days, we'll assess the situation."

Elaina didn't like the sound of that last comment. "What does that mean?"

He lifted his shoulder. "My job is in San Antonio. If the security threat is removed, if you're free to leave Crystal Creek, then maybe you can move back into the city so you can see Christopher more often."

Her heart sank. That arrangement wasn't nearly enough. "I don't want to just be able to see him. I want to be his mother."

"Trust me, this isn't easy for me to say. You *are* his mother."

Elaina couldn't imagine being more shocked. She stood there. Speechless. It was a huge concession coming from a man who just an hour earlier had accused her of participating in an illegal adoption.

Luke groaned and leaned his back against the wall. "When we were at the sitter's, Christopher went right to you. He smiled at you. It's obvious he loves you, and I can't completely discount that." His eyes met hers. The gray color turned to steel, and his expression hardened. "Just don't give me a reason to."

Elaina hoped she didn't look too guilty, because, after all, she had been thinking about leaving that night. But that was before she saw how much Luke already loved Christopher. If she took the little boy, Luke would come after her. With his contacts and experience, he'd no doubt find her, too. And he'd have her arrested. She wouldn't stand a chance of being part of Christopher's life if she was behind bars.

"I won't give you a reason to cut me out of Christopher's life," she promised.

Elaina hoped it was a promise she could keep.

The doorbell rang, and that had Luke reaching for his gun again. It also had her heart racing out of control. Before Luke had stormed into her life, she'd managed to find a small sense of security.

That was all gone now.

Feeling safe might be a thing she'd never experience again. His gun and mere presence were reminders of that.

"Are you expecting anyone?" Luke asked.

She shook her head, and Luke followed her when she went to see who it was. Elaina looked out the door scope. The person on the other side certainly wasn't the threat that her body had prepared itself for. She recognized the lanky man with the mop of unruly ginger-colored hair.

"It's Gary Simpson. My neighbor."

That didn't cause Luke to relax one bit. He still kept a firm grip on his gun. "He comes by often?"

"Yes." Elaina refrained from adding *too often.* "He probably saw my car and is checking on me because I'm not usually home this time of day. Or else he heard about the men who were arrested in front of Theresa's house. If I don't answer the door, he'll get suspicious."

Luke waited a moment, as if deciding what to do with that information, and then reholstered his gun. He tipped his head to the door, an indication for her to open it.

Elaina did, after she temporarily deactivated the security system. She wanted to do everything possible to make certain this wasn't a long visit. Her goal was to put Gary's concerns and questions to rest so she could get rid of him.

Gary was about to ring the bell again, but he stopped when he saw her. "Elaina."

That was the only greeting her neighbor provided,

but his cautious blue eyes immediately landed on Luke. He didn't have to look far to see him because Luke quickly joined her. Side-by-side. He even slipped his arm around her waist, a reminder that this was showtime. He wanted them to go into their couple routine.

"It's true then," Gary said. "Your husband came home."

"I did," Luke volunteered.

And there was definitely something territorial about the way Luke said it. The embrace was territorial, as well, and he pulled her even closer to him.

Gary's reaction wasn't exactly passive, either. His too-full mouth tightened, and he shoved his hands into the pockets of jeans, but not before Elaina noticed that his hands had fisted.

She knew that Gary was attracted to her. After all, he'd asked her out several times. Not for real dates, he'd said, but invitations to join him for steaks that he was barbecuing. Or for a swim in his pool. Elaina had always declined and then flashed her fake wedding ring to remind him that she wasn't available. But judging from his expression, Gary wanted to believe differently.

"Elaina, are you…okay?" Gary asked.

His hesitant question had more than a tinge of suspicion to it. Maybe because despite the embrace with Luke, she didn't look like a loving wife whose missing husband had just returned to her.

Her lack of sincerity would no doubt rile Luke if

he thought she wasn't doing her best to play her part, so she immediately tried to do just that. Elaina looked up at Luke and hoped she had love in her eyes. Fake love, of course.

Luke looked down at her at the same moment that Elaina looked up. He was doing the fake love act, too, but he was obviously a lot better at it than she was. His eyes softened. The corner of his mouth lifted. And he smiled. He probably didn't know that his smile was his best feature. He was handsome with the stone face, but with that smile, he was in whole different category of handsome.

Okay, he was hot.

Elaina hated that she had to admit that, especially since she was doing her best to forget anything remotely positive about him. But it didn't matter. In the grand scheme of things, good looks meant nothing.

"Elaina?" she heard Gary say.

She forced her attention away from Luke. "I'm fine," she answering, trying to smile. It didn't come as easily for her as it did Luke.

"Are you sure, because you—"

"She's fine," Luke interrupted. He leaned in and brushed that smiling mouth over hers.

It was a simple gesture. An act. But Elaina felt herself go all tingly and warm. Heck, she even felt it all the way to her toes. Furious at her reaction, she dismissed it as fatigue and fear. Or at least that's what she tried to do, but Luke didn't take his mouth from hers. The tingling and warmth soon began to skyrocket.

She pinched his back and would have pinched herself if she hadn't thought it would make Gary even more wary.

Luke reacted to the pinch. He pulled away and stared down at her. He looked stunned. Or something. And he shook his head as if he couldn't believe what had just happened. Maybe that's because he might have experienced it, too.

"I'm fine," Elaina repeated to Gary. "Really. Couldn't be better." And she put an unspoken "goodbye" at the end of that.

"Good. That's good." Gary nodded awkwardly. He obviously didn't catch the goodbye part because he continued. "I heard about the protestors. The sheriff's holding them for questioning or something. There's also a federal agent of some kind down at the jail, but the sheriff sure isn't saying anything about why he's there."

Well, it'd taken less than an hour for that information to make it to Gary, which meant it was all over town. Hopefully, it would keep most folks from visiting because they'd probably think she wanted to spend some time alone with her *husband*. Being alone with Luke was no piece of cake. Her body couldn't take much more of this.

Elaina decided to go for the direct approach. "I'll see you soon," she said to Gary. She waited until he issued an unenthusiastic goodbye before she shut the door.

Luke didn't let go of her.

She didn't let go of him.

They just stood there with his arm still curved around her waist.

"This is a lot harder than I thought it'd be," Luke mumbled.

"Welcome to the club."

She paused, trying to figure out how to say what she needed to say. Elaina finally decided to heck with it. This was something that had to be said. But Elaina didn't continue until she stepped from his embrace and put some distance between them. "We dislike each other. But you're still a man, and I'm a woman. Our bodies aren't reacting as if we're enemies."

He nodded. "Our bodies were reacting to the adrenaline."

Elaina toyed with that explanation and figured it was a good one. She only wished she'd thought of it first.

Even more, she wished it were totally true.

"Just in case it's a little more than that," she added, "I'm going to suggest no more kisses."

His eyebrow came up. "You're probably right. Besides, we have enough to deal with without adding adrenaline reactions to the mix."

Elaina had no trouble agreeing with that.

Luke reached over and reactivated the security system. Since he pressed in the correct code, he must have watched her before she opened the door for Gary.

"Do you think your neighbor is suspicious that I'm not your husband?" Luke asked.

"No. He's jealous. I don't think anyone in town

suspects that you aren't Daniel Allen. If they did, we would have already heard about it."

"Good. Let's keep it that way." He propped his hands on his hips and glanced around the room. "We need to make sure all the windows and doors are locked. And close the blinds."

He didn't wait for her to comply; he started the task by checking the windows in the living room. "After we're done, stay away from the windows and don't go back outside."

All of his activity got her heart racing. "Wait a minute. Those men are still in jail, aren't they?"

Luke snared her gaze, and Elaina saw it then. Not the attraction. Not the cockiness. Definitely not the "loving husband" he'd been just moments earlier.

She saw the concern.

"Those men are in jail," Luke confirmed. He turned toward Christopher's room and said the rest of what he had to say over his shoulder as he walked away. "But that doesn't mean they're working alone."

Chapter Six

Luke was practically soaking wet, but he didn't care. He wasn't about to leave his son's bath time just so he could dry off.

Christopher was enjoying himself in what was left of the two inches of warm water inside his little yellow plastic tub. Elaina had placed that tub inside the regular porcelain one in the bathroom. At first, Luke hadn't understood why she did that. But after watching Christopher splash water over Elaina, Luke, himself and most of the entire room, he knew this was the best place for his son.

He wondered how long it would take him to learn all the little things that made Christopher's life happier and safer. Feeding him dinner had been an enjoyable challenge, but those challenges were just starting.

Luke smiled at that.

Then, frowned.

He'd never felt more incompetent at anything in his life. And yet, he'd never looked so forward to anything, either. Through the baths, feedings and playtimes, he'd get to know his baby, they'd form a bond, and he'd no longer be a father in name only.

"He's a special little boy, isn't he?" Luke heard Elaina say.

Luke turned toward her. She was watching him watch Christopher, and the pain and doubts were there all over her face. A huge contrast to the laughing, splashing baby in the tub.

"He's usually happy like this?" he asked.

She smiled, just a brief one, before she clamped it off. "Most of the time. But he'll get sleepy soon, and then he's likely to be cranky."

Luke checked his watch. It was nearly 8:00 p.m., which meant his son would soon be going to bed. That would leave Luke alone with Elaina. When he'd come up with this plan, he certainly hadn't realized that the hardest part wouldn't be dealing with his son, but with the woman who'd raised him.

"You won't change his name, will you?" Elaina asked.

It seemed an odd question, but after giving it some thought, maybe it wasn't so odd. He certainly hadn't had any say in anything to do with Christopher— including something this important. "You named him?"

"Yes. Christopher Sean. He's not named after anyone. It's just something I liked. So, there's no baggage or relatives attached to it if that's what you thought."

He hadn't thought that at all. Luke had done a

thorough background check on Elaina, and neither of those names had come up.

"Christopher suits him," Luke concluded. "The only thing that'll change is his surname."

"That doesn't matter," she mumbled. "It's fake anyway. As you pointed out, my entire life is fake."

That wasn't true. What his son felt for her was real, and even Luke couldn't dismiss that.

Christopher reached for her, batting her hand with the rubber duck he was clutching. She smiled and tickled him on his belly. Christopher giggled and splashed some more.

Elaina caught the brunt of the water this time. Christopher doused the front of her clingy, garnet-red top. The water made it even more clingy, and that was Luke's cue to get his attention off her clothes and the way they fit her body.

"Just to let you know," Luke said, going over the ground rules. "We'll be sleeping in the nursery tonight with Christopher."

She froze a moment, shook her head as if ready to disagree with that, but then her eyes widened. "You mean because of the danger? Well, I'd planned on sleeping next to him anyway. I figured you'd take the sofa in the living room."

"Not a chance of that." He caught on to one of Christopher toes and played a silent game of Little Piggy. Christopher grinned from ear to ear.

Elaina didn't grin. She frowned. "Then, I'll take the sofa. You can stay with Christopher."

She obviously didn't understand that these were rules, not suggestions. "No one is going to take the sofa. We're all going to sleep in the same room because it's the only way I can make sure both of you are safe."

That improved her posture. Her shoulders went back, and he got a better view of what the water had done to her top, the way it clung to her breasts. Man, he could see the outline of nipples.

"You think gunmen are going to storm the house?" Elaina asked.

It took a second to gather his breath. Nipples! "I think I don't want to take a chance like that," he countered.

She handed Christopher his toy duck when it floated out of his reach. "You've seen the nursery, and you know it's not big enough for both of us."

He wasn't sure a shopping mall was big enough for both of them. "You're wasting your time with this argument. We're staying in the nursery. I'm doing this for your own good. For your *safety.*"

"But who'll protect us from each other?" she mumbled. But then, Elaina immediately waved that off. "Don't answer that. I don't want to know."

Too bad. It suddenly seemed like a critical subject. Or at least an interesting one. "Maybe we should address it. The attraction," he clarified just to make sure they were on the same page.

"The only reason to address it is to dismiss it. I'm not getting involved with another man. Especially a man who has the power to destroy me."

He found her honesty refreshing, and his attitude had nothing to do with her top. Or her nipples. Or her snug jeans. Or her bare feet with their peach painted toenails. Or even her scent.

Okay, maybe it did have something to do with those things. But Luke vowed that he wouldn't let his stupid male body make bad decisions for him.

"Kevin left you with a bitter taste in your mouth," he commented to keep the conversation going. It was better than the silence. He did a second round of the Little Piggy game with Christopher.

"Oh, yes. But then, you can probably say the same thing. After all, you were separated when your wife died."

Touché. "It'd gone beyond that," he confessed. Why, he didn't know. He just suddenly felt the need to spill his guts to the one woman who didn't care one iota about what he'd been through. "Taylor had filed for a divorce."

She studied him, and he could almost see the wheels working in her head. "Yet she didn't tell you that she was pregnant."

"Nope. She didn't. But then, Taylor never wanted kids. That's one of the reasons we decided to go our separate ways."

Her stare softened a bit. No more visual accusations. "You wanted to have children?"

"For as long as I can remember." For some reason, he wanted to blather on about this part, too. Maybe the bath water had soaked his brain. "My parents died in a car accident when I was three, and I was raised in foster care. *Bad* foster care," he added. "I always wanted a chance to experience a good family life. Taylor, though, wanted the opposite. She'd had a rough childhood, too, and felt she couldn't be a good mother."

Elaina stayed quiet a moment. "Do you think she was planning to give up Christopher for adoption?"

He wanted to shout a resounding no, but he couldn't. Because Luke honestly didn't know the answer to that. "Maybe. Another of our big areas of disagreement was my job. She said it was too dangerous, but she didn't want me to quit because she liked all the traveling I did. It gave her some space, as she used to like to say."

"So, maybe she was planning on giving up her baby to keep that *space?*" she asked.

"Either that, or she reasoned that because of my dangerous job, I wouldn't make a good father." This time, Luke retrieved Christopher's duck. "What Taylor didn't know was that I was up for a promotion that would essentially mean a desk job. I got that promotion, but within the same hour I learned that Taylor was dead."

Elaina made a soft sound of sympathy. "If Taylor planned to give up your baby, then the adoption might have been legal."

Ah, so that's where this was going. Luke didn't let it go far. So much for pouring out his heart and spilling his guts. Elaina had taken all those bits of info so she could try to clear her conscience.

"Taylor's intentions might have made that part of it legal, but the paperwork and the process weren't." He stared at her. "Do you have any doubts that your late fiancé was capable of an illegal adoption?"

"No," she said, but the admission was laced with frustration. "In hindsight, I think Kevin was capable of just about anything." She aimed her finger at him. "I won't go through that again, and that's why this attraction thing between us won't go any further."

Luke didn't doubt the smoldering glances he'd been giving Elaina, but he hadn't noticed Elaina sending any his way. Of course, he was aware of the uncomfortable tension between them.

"How do I know the attraction is real on your part?" he asked. "You could be faking it."

She looked genuinely surprised and offended. "And why would I do that?"

"Because you think it'll help your cause."

"My *cause?*"

Luke figured he was about to put his foot directly into his big mouth. "You must be trying to figure a way to keep custody of Christopher."

Yep. Definitely foot in mouth. Her eyes narrowed, and her mouth tightened. "I'm so glad you said that, because it reminds me of why I dislike you. Not everyone has ulterior motives for what they do, Luke Buchanan. Trust me, I had my fill of that kind of stuff when I was with Kevin."

Christopher started to make fussing noises, and he rubbed his eyes. Elaina jumped to her feet, grabbed a towel and scooped him up in it. "Bed time," she announced.

Well, there were definitely no more smoldering looks between them, and the air had chilled. She turned her back on him and went into the nursery.

"He won't like this part," she grumbled as she placed Christopher on the dressing table.

Learning from his mistake, Luke shut up and watched her diaper the baby. Though he considered himself a smart man, he figured that would take a while to master the technique and all the steps. Christopher wiggled, squirmed, fussed and generally did everything but cooperate. Yet, Elaina managed to get the baby dressed for bed in only a couple of minutes.

She kissed Christopher on both of his chubby cheeks and lay him in the bed. She covered him with the quilt and began to hum softly. Luke recognized the tune: "Lullaby and Goodnight." While she hummed it, she lightly rubbed the baby's stomach. Like the dressing routine, it only took a couple of minutes before Christopher closed his eyes.

Since there was a night light in the corner of the room, Luke turned off the overhead light. He made his way to the window to look out, to check the yard one more time. He'd lost count of just how many times he'd done that in the course of the afternoon and the evening.

He'd check many more times throughout the night.

"See anything?" Elaina whispered.

"No. It's all clear."

Christopher was no doubt asleep because she moved away from the crib. "I'm exhausted. I'm going to try to get some sleep."

It was early, but Luke knew how she felt. It'd been a long day, and even with the extreme fatigue, neither of them would get much sleep.

She walked toward the hall. "I'll get some pillows and blankets for us."

She disappeared into her bedroom, and because that didn't seem an appropriate place for him to be, Luke stayed put and looked down at his now sleeping son. It was hard to imagine that the little boy who'd been a ball of energy just minutes earlier was now sleeping so peacefully. Luke wanted to make sure things stayed peaceful.

Elaina returned to the nursery and deposited an armful of bedding on the carpeted floor. With her arms free, Luke could see that she'd changed her clothes. Nothing provocative. She wore cream-colored flannel pajamas. But it was still somehow intimate to be in the same room with her while she was preparing for bed.

With the uncomfortable silence, Luke had time to go over everything they'd discussed, and the one thing he kept returning to was Kevin. Was Elaina's ex the reason those men had come to Crystal Creek? If so, what was the way to make the connection, especially if the two men weren't in a talkative mood during the interviews?

"You said that Kevin was doing some kind of

software modification," Luke whispered. "Was it legal?"

"Probably not." She spread out the covers and tossed him a pillow. "In fact, I'd be shocked if it was."

Luke placed the pillow on the floor, but since the room was indeed small, his pillow was less than two feet from where Elaina's was. "If Kevin was that bad, then why'd you get involved with him in the first place?"

"We were college sweethearts. I didn't learn about his criminal activities until he was dead and I started going through his things." She settled into her make-shift bed. "It was like he was two different people. Despite bouts of manic depression, he was usually kind and generous with me. But to the rest of the world, well, he was a scumbag."

Luke made a mental note to learn just how much of a scumbag Kevin was.

"Who hired Kevin to do these software modifications?" Luke asked.

"I don't know. He only referred to his boss as T. I don't know if T was a man or a woman, and I certainly have no idea what the person's real name is. But I do know that the modifications were important. Kevin spent a lot of time doing them, and he said it was a project that would make us millionaires several times over."

Interesting. A big project worth a lot of money. "You believed him?"

"Yes. He'd never said anything like that before.

And before he was killed, he made some rather large deposits into our investment accounts."

Well, that added some credence to Kevin's claims. "How was he doing these modifications?"

"He put everything on a miniature memory card."

That wasn't something Luke wanted to hear. There were memory cards half the size of a dime and just as thin. "Did you bring anything with you when you left San Antonio?"

She turned slightly to make eye contact. "Just some files, investment account statements and the adoption papers. I brought some of Christopher's toys, of course. And his car seat. Oh, and I also brought the clothes and blanket he was wrapped in the day I first saw him."

"That was the day Kevin brought Christopher home to you?" Luke asked.

She nodded.

And here he had been on a case while another man was essentially stealing his child. Luke knew he'd never forgive himself for that. All he could do was make the world a little safer for Christopher.

"Kevin was killed only hours after he handed me the baby," Elaina added.

Yeah. Luke knew that, and he'd come to the conclusion that Kevin hadn't had the miniature disk with him. If he had, those men likely wouldn't have come after Elaina.

"How about a computer?" Luke pressed. "Did you bring one to Crystal Creek with you?"

"My laptop, but Kevin never used it."

Perhaps not when she was around, but Luke knew Kevin still could have used it. "I'd like to see the files, the clothing and the laptop."

She stared at him, and for a moment he thought she might refuse. But then Elaina huffed, got up and indicated for him to follow her. Where did they go?

Her bedroom.

The last place on earth he should be.

Luke wanted to hit himself in the head with a rock for such a blunder, but he needed to see what Elaina had brought with her to Crystal Creek. It could help them figure out what was going on.

The room had been painted the color of fresh butter, and the bedding was a floral print with that same yellow and some mint green. There was very little furniture. Sparse but comfortable. In the short months that she'd been in the house, she'd turned it into a home.

"There's the computer," she said, pointing to the laptop on the small desk tucked in the corner.

Luke glanced at it while Elaina went to the walk-in closet. There was a small attic space just above the top shelf, and she stood on a footstool to reach the hatch door. When she reached up, her pajama top rose, and he got a great look at her bare midriff.

He forced himself to look elsewhere.

Unfortunately, elsewhere turned out to be her butt. Lifting her arms and standing on her tiptoes adjusted the fabric, as well, and he got an intimate view of the outline of her derriere. Great. He hoped that was the last of the torturing peepshow.

His body laughed at him for hoping that and begged to see more. Luke didn't fulfill that wish. He nailed his attention to Elaina's hands, figuring he couldn't get in mental trouble with those.

He watched as she took out a small cardboard box. It definitely wasn't in plain view, and she'd likely done that on purpose. She probably hadn't wanted anyone to learn of Christopher's adoption or Kevin's activities.

She deposited the box on the desk next to him. When she didn't say anything, Luke looked up at her to see if anything was wrong.

"Your shirt," she said. "I hadn't realized it was so wet."

Luke glanced down and verified the wetness on his white button-down shirt. It was like her own top in the bathroom. Clingy. "I'll change it in a few minutes."

And then he remembered, he'd left his suitcase in his car at the parking lot of Elaina's shop. Her expression said that she remembered even if he hadn't.

"This shirt will dry," he grumbled.

He made a mental note to get his suitcase when he went to the jail for the interviews. For that, Rusty and he would have to trade places, with his fellow agent staying with Christopher and Elaina. Luke didn't want either of them anywhere near that jail with those two men.

Of course, Luke's presence at the jail would mean

a lot of questions from the locals, but he'd have to deal with it somehow. He couldn't miss those interviews.

"These are the clothes Christopher was wearing when he came from the adoption agency," Elaina said, taking a blue gown, a knit pom-pom cap and satin-rimmed blanket from the box. The gown and hat were tiny, and he couldn't help but wonder how his son had ever fit into them.

Luke sat down at the desk and turned on her laptop. While it was booting up, he looked at what she handed him. Yeah, they were baby clothes all right. He put them closer to his nose and inhaled. It was probably his imagination, but he thought he could still detect his son's scent.

He also suddenly became aware that Elaina was staring at him. Luke looked at her, figuring she would have a good laugh about a grown man sniffing baby clothes, but she didn't. In fact, her eyes got a little misty.

"There's more," she said, clearing her throat.

She handed him the adoption papers. Unlike the clothes, he had no desire to sniff these. In fact, they made his blood boil. Because these were the documents the criminals had used to sell his son to the highest bidder.

The papers looked perfectly legal, right down to the official gold seal on the top document, but Luke knew they were phony. The documents had basically been created by an attorney who wanted to get rich. No rules had been followed, and no legal official had given it that seal of approval.

Luke thumbed through the papers, and the only signature he saw was Kevin's. "You weren't there when these papers were signed?"

She shook her head. "No. In fact, I didn't really know what Kevin was up to. He'd mentioned an adoption, of course, but I figured it'd take months or even years. Then, just a few days later, he showed up with Christopher."

"You weren't suspicious?" he asked.

"Of course. But Kevin said that adoption happened faster because it was private and he was willing to pay more to expedite the paperwork."

Yet more proof that it was illegal.

Not that Luke needed more.

While Elaina sat on the edge of her bed, Luke surfed through her computer. He didn't immediately find anything out of place, but then, he wasn't a computer expert.

"How did you get the money to buy this house and pay the lease for your shop?" Luke asked when he didn't find any financial records. In fact, the only thing he did find was art software that she'd obviously been using to create her stained-glass designs.

"I had some money in an investment account that I set up when I sold my condo in San Antonio," she explained. "I also sold some jewelry. None of the pieces were distinctive or unique enough so I didn't think anyone who saw them would associate them with me. I didn't touch the joint accounts I had with

Kevin because I thought it'd create a paper trail that would lead those men to me."

"It would have," Luke mumbled. "I'd like to send this laptop to the Justice Department."

"Okay. I use it to keep track of my Internet orders, but if you think it'll help, send it. I've already got my files backed up on my jump drive." She tipped her head to the thumb-size memory stick and then paused. In fact, she paused so long that Luke looked at her to see what was wrong. "We'll be safe here, right?"

He certainly couldn't doubt the sincerity of that question. Nor could he doubt that concern in her voice. "As long as those men are in jail."

She wadded up the quilt in her hands, squeezed hard and then got up to pace. "But if you can't keep them there, then what?"

There was no way to sugarcoat this. "We'll have to leave. I'm trying to avoid that, of course. For Christopher's sake."

Elaina nodded. A shaky nod. "I'm tired. You can send any of the things in that box to the Justice Department, but when they're finished with them, I'd like to have the clothes back." She walked away.

That was obviously a good-night, and Elaina probably thought he'd sit in her room and pore over the papers. But he wouldn't. He didn't want to leave Christopher or her alone while he did that. So, he followed her.

She glanced over her shoulder, and even though the hall was dark, he was pretty sure she rolled her eyes.

"We can't avoid this," he whispered as they entered the nursery. "I'm sleeping in here with you."

She turned around so quickly that he bumped right into her. In fact, his hands were suddenly filled with her. She was soft. And warm. And she smelled damn good. Not like cherries, this time. It was mix of baby shampoo and the spicy pasta dish she'd fixed for dinner. Normally, he wouldn't have found that combination erotic, but he certainly thought so now.

Of course, he also thought he was acting like a fool.

Elaina didn't stay in his arms long. Mere seconds. The night light provided the only illumination in the room, but he had no trouble seeing her expression. She was frowning and nibbling on her lip at the same time.

"I'm warning you, I snore," she snarled.

If that was the worst thing he had to face, then that would suit him just fine. But Luke wasn't very hopeful.

There were way too many things that could go wrong tonight.

Chapter Seven

Elaina dreamed. It was the nightmare again. A race against time, armed men and other terrifying shadowy things that could harm her baby. She would dodge one shadow, only to be faced with another.

One of those shadows was Luke Buchanan.

Even in the depth of the dream, she knew he was the greatest threat of all. She could run from the men. She could hide. But she couldn't escape a biological father who wanted to raise his son.

She stirred, trying to force that painful thought aside, and she opened her eyes. The first thing she saw and felt was Luke. He was there. Right next to her. In fact, they were on their sides facing each other. Well, rather she had her face right against his bare chest. Sometime during the night, he'd obviously removed his shirt.

And she'd cuddled right up to him.

And there was no mistake about it, this was cuddling. Body against body.

Just as she'd expected, his body was toned and perfect. He was all strength and muscles, and he smelled warm, musky and male. It was a dangerous combination that had her pushing aside the nightmare and remembering things that she hadn't even realized she missed.

Like French kisses and sex.

Things that weren't going to happen between Luke Buchanan and her.

Elaina scrambled away from him and winced when she banged her foot on the baby bed. It was loud, and maybe because the room had been so quiet, the noise seemed to echo.

The noise created a simple chain reaction. Luke woke up. Not a slow, drowsy wake up, either. His eyes shot open, and in the same motion he reached for his gun on the floor next to him. His attention sliced around the room, and he relaxed when he realized there was no threat.

Christopher woke up, too. Not quietly, either. He let out a baby howl, and he sat up. He used the bed railings to pull himself to a standing position.

Luke and she got up at the same time to reach for the baby. She won, only because she was closer. She scooped Christopher into her arms and tried to soothe him with a kiss which didn't work.

Elaina checked the clock and realized why. It was well past 8:00 a.m., which meant it was well past his breakfast time.

How could she have possibly overslept with Luke

in the room? And then she remembered. It'd been the wee hours of the morning before she'd been able to fall asleep. She knew for a fact that it was the same for Luke, because he was still awake when she'd finally drifted off.

"He's hungry," she grumbled.

Normally, she would have put Christopher in his high chair while she fixed his breakfast. But then, normally her baby wasn't crying. The late start had thrown everything off schedule.

"I'll take him," Luke said obviously sensing her dilemma.

"I figured you'd need to get dressed and go the sheriff's office for the interrogations." In other words—*leave,* Elaina tried to convey.

"There's no need to go in until the lawyer arrives. Rusty will call when that happens." Luke reached for Christopher again.

"He'll need to have his diaper changed first," Elaina informed him.

Luke blinked, but the hesitation didn't last long. "I'll do it."

Elaina hesitated, as well, but Christopher's tears helped her with a quick decision. She handed the baby to Luke and headed for the kitchen.

While she fixed baby oatmeal in the microwave, she listened for any sounds that Luke was in over his head. Christopher stopped crying, and it was because of the near silence that she heard Luke make an odd sound. Elaina raced back toward the nursery.

By the time she made it there, her mind was already ripe with possibilities as to what had caused Luke to make that noise. Bad possibilities. But all she saw was Christopher on the changing table. He was smiling and kicking his legs. Luke's chest, however, was wet.

"He's got good aim," Luke mumbled.

Elaina couldn't help it, she laughed. "I should have warned you about the hazards of diapering a baby boy. He's peed on me more than a time or two."

The corner of Luke's mouth lifted, and they shared a smile. Along with Christopher's happy gurglings, the moment turned a little weird. It was too intimate. As if they were a family. Which they weren't.

The happy moment ended as quickly as it'd come.

"I'll get back to making breakfast," she told Luke. "You might want to use the baby wipes to clean yourself."

Feeling awkward and warm at the same time, Elaina made her way back to the kitchen to finish the oatmeal. What was wrong with her anyway? She'd started the morning thinking about French kisses and sex. Now, she was thinking about family. Talk about insane notions.

Or was it?

She was almost afraid to let the thought fully materialize in her head, but she couldn't seem to stop it, either. After all, it was Luke who wanted to pretend to be a loving, happy couple. For Christopher's sake. But what was wrong with continuing that pretense until they could figure out what to do about shared custody and such?

Plus, there were the men in jail. Having Luke around would mean that Christopher would be safe, because Elaina knew he would protect his son.

Of course, the downside to having Luke around was that she was starting to feel things that she thought she'd never feel again. Feelings she'd buried with Kevin.

Feelings that Luke would never be able to feel for her in return.

To him, she was the enemy. She was the woman who'd robbed him of all these months with his son. The only feelings that Luke would ever have for her would be part of this pretense.

And that was okay.

Elaina repeated that to herself.

She already had enough to deal with without adding feelings and emotions to the mix.

By the time Luke and Christopher joined her in the kitchen, Elaina was reasonably sure that her little talk with herself was working. She was getting her mind back on the right things. Then, she saw Luke's bare chest, watched him lovingly put Christopher in his high chair and she needed another attitude adjustment.

It was going to be a *long* day.

Luke had just sat down to start feeding Christopher the oatmeal when his cell phone rang. Elaina took over the feeding duties while he took the call.

"Hello, Rusty," he answered after glancing at his Caller ID.

Elaina divided her attention between feeding Christopher and watching Luke's reaction. She knew the call could be important, but judging from Luke's tight jaw, something had gone wrong. Unfortunately, she couldn't tell what.

Other than simple yes and no responses, she did hear Luke request a "safe house" which sent a shiver of panic through her. Did he honestly think they needed something like that? Unfortunately, Elaina had to wait until he'd finished the call before she could get an explanation.

"That was Rusty who's down at the sheriff's office," Luke relayed to her. "He said he'll drop off my suitcase this morning so I won't have to leave you to drive over there."

She studied him. "Then, why are you scowling?"

"Well, it's not because of the suitcase. The lawyer's been delayed. He won't be in Crystal Creek until tomorrow afternoon at the earliest. That means the interviews aren't going to happen until then."

She scowled then, too. She wanted this over and done, and that couldn't happen until the men gave up some information.

"And the safe house?" Elaina asked. "What was that all about?"

"A precaution. I asked Rusty to request a safe house just in case we have to release those men tomorrow. I don't want Christopher or you here with them loose."

Neither did Elaina. But then, a safe house seemed a little extreme. Unless… "Does this mean you think the men will be released?"

Luke shrugged. "We have reason to hold them, so I don't think they're going anywhere, but we have to be prepared, just in case." He leaned against the counter and watched her feed Christopher. "There's also the likelihood that these men aren't working alone."

"Yes," she said, feeling that panic again. "They could be working for T."

"It's also possible that one of the men could be T," Luke quickly pointed out.

Elaina prayed that was true, because if so, that meant the threat was contained. Too bad she didn't know how long that would last.

There was a soft knock at the door. Because she'd been deep in thought about the threat, she embarrassed herself by gasping.

Luke took the knock seriously, too. He hurried to the bedroom and retrieved his shirt and gun before he went to the front door and looked out the peephole.

"It's not my neighbor, Gary, is it?" Elaina whispered.

"No. It's two women." He slipped on his shirt. "One of them is your assistant, Carrie."

No more panicked feeling, but Elaina was a little concerned. Carrie wasn't in the habit of dropping by for an early morning visit. That was especially true since her assistant no doubt thought she was on what was essentially a second honeymoon.

Elaina sprinkled some dry cereal bits onto Christopher's tray so that it would keep him occupied, and she joined Luke at the door. She glanced out and saw not only Carrie but Brenda McQueen, a frequent visitor to the shop. Both women looked apprehensive.

"The other woman is a customer," Elaina explained.

"You know her well?"

Elaina shrugged. "Not really. Her name is Brenda McQueen. She moved here a couple of months ago, and she works out of her home as the editor of a children's magazine."

"I didn't run a background check on her," he mumbled. "But I will."

Her first instinct was to say that wasn't necessary, but Elaina no longer knew what was necessary or not.

"I'll see what they want," Elaina told Luke. She disengaged the security system so that it wouldn't go off when she opened the door.

Luke tucked his gun in the back waist of his pants and stepped to the side so she could face their visitors.

"Elaina," Carrie greeted. Her voice was strained, as was her expression.

Both women stood there. Carrie, in a pair of jeans and a blue hoodie. Brenda wore black sweatpants and a Duke sweatshirt that brought out the blue in her eyes. The winter wind whipped at Brenda's midnight-black hair that she'd gathered into a loose ponytail, and it would have done the same for Carrie's if she hadn't been wearing a French braid.

Carrie glanced at Luke who was standing just behind Elaina. "I'm so sorry to bother you—"

"I insisted that we come," Brenda interjected. "I was out for my morning jog and saw that the front door of your shop was open."

Sweet heaven. What else could go wrong?

"I locked it before I left work," Carrie insisted.

"Why don't you come in," Luke offered.

Elaina followed Luke's gaze to see why he'd said that, and she quickly noticed that he had his attention fastened on Gary, her neighbor. Gary had his Golden Retriever on a leash and was walking the dog on the sidewalk just in front of Elaina's house.

Or rather, Gary was lingering with the dog.

Luke obviously didn't trust the man. Elaina knew how he felt. She was beginning to not trust *anyone*.

"Nothing is missing from the shop," Carrie volunteered as they stepped inside. Luke shut the door and buttoned his shirt. But not before both visitors eyed his chest.

Elaina knew how they felt.

She'd done some eyeing herself.

"The lock wasn't broken, either," Carrie continued. She went to Christopher and gave his cheek a pinch, but the cheerfulness of the gesture wasn't present in any part of her body language. "I guess it's possible that I didn't fully close the door when I locked up, but I could have sworn I did."

"We were going to report it to the sheriff," Brenda added. "But since nothing appears to be stolen, we wanted to check with you first, just to make sure you weren't the one who'd left it open."

"I'll take care of it," Luke insisted before Elaina could say anything.

Brenda stared at him, and that's when Elaina realized that she'd failed to make introductions. "Brenda, this is, uh, my husband, Daniel."

"Obviously," the woman said, her mouth bending into a smile. She directed her comments to Luke. "I'll bet you're not so happy about us bursting in here like this. I hope we didn't interrupt anything too personal."

"We were just feeding Christopher," Elaina said because she didn't know what else to say.

That seemed to be Luke's cue to slip his arm around her waist. Elaina didn't fight it. In fact, she felt herself leaning into the embrace.

Carrie leaned down and kissed Christopher on the top of his head. "Brenda, we should be going."

"Absolutely." But the woman didn't head for the door. Instead, she pulled Elaina aside and whispered in her ear. "I think I might have started my period, and I don't have anything with me."

Oh. So, it wasn't anything huge. Elaina was getting weary of the huge stuff. "You'll find some *supplies* in the master bathroom," Elaina whispered back. "Under the sink."

Brenda thanked her and disappeared down the hall. Elaina welcomed the reprieve. She liked Brenda, but she wanted a minute with Carrie. Obviously, so did Luke.

"Did it look as if someone had picked the lock on the shop door?" he asked Carrie.

"No. I checked for scratches or some kind of marks but nothing. I'm so sorry this happened, Elaina—"

"You don't have to apologize. That shop door is old, and I should have had it checked months ago."

And she hoped that was all there was to it. An old door with an old lock. Elaina didn't want to think about an intruder. Or what an intruder might have been looking for inside her place of business.

"Would you like me to take Christopher today? I could drive him to the sitter's or take him to the shop." Carrie asked. "You two must want some alone time."

"We'll get our alone time," Elaina insisted. Besides, she didn't want Christopher anywhere outside until Luke had been able to confirm that there'd been no break-in.

"Were you with Brenda when she discovered the shop door open?" Luke continued.

"No. She called me on her cell phone. I was still at home. She knew you had gone home, and Brenda wasn't sure if she should interrupt you guys."

That sounded plausible, but Luke didn't look as if he totally bought the explanation. Of course, they were both suspicious of almost everyone.

"I noticed Gary outside," Carrie commented. She blinked and lightly rubbed her right eye.

Elaina nodded. "He came by yesterday afternoon."

Carrie offered a flat, dry smile. "Let me guess. He wasn't that enthusiastic to see Daniel here."

"No, he wasn't," Luke provided.

"He'll get over it. I swear, Elaina never gave him any encouragement. Just the opposite. She was always telling everyone how much she was in love with you."

It was another of those awkward moments.

Because Christopher started to fuss, Elaina moved out of Luke's embrace so she could finish feeding him his oatmeal. It was a welcome reprieve.

Carrie checked her watch. "Brenda needs to hurry. I have to get to the shop. The woman from Luling is coming by this morning to pick up that Victorian panel."

"Do you need me there for that?" Elaina asked.

"Not on your life. You're staying here with your husband. I insist. Remember, I don't want to see your face in that shop for at least a week."

Elaina had no intentions of being gone that long. But then, it wasn't easy to think of the future, mainly because she had no idea what her future held.

Brenda came back into the room and she immediately grabbed Carrie's hand. "Let's get out of here and leave these two lovebirds alone."

But Carrie pulled out of her grip. She blinked hard again. "There's something underneath my contact, and it's bothering me. I won't be long." And she rushed off to the bathroom.

Brenda looked at Luke and smiled nervously. "The whole town is talking about you, you know. Everyone is anxious to meet you. Don't worry though, they'll stay away for another day or two. Will you stay in the military?" Brenda asked.

It wasn't something Luke and she had rehearsed, though thankfully he had an answer. "No. I'm on what they call terminal leave right now. I should receive papers soon that'll release me from active duty."

Brenda studied him. "I don't guess you want to talk about being held captive?"

"No," Elaina and Luke said in unison.

"I understand." Brenda paused. "I know you're just trying to get your footing, but I hope you won't take Elaina and Christopher away from us."

"We haven't made a decision about where we'll live," Elaina provided. And she kept her tone a little cool so that it would hopefully prevent any more questions.

It worked. Well, that and the fact that Carrie came back into the room. Carrie gave Christopher another kiss and then followed Brenda out the door. Luke didn't waste any time locking it and resetting the security system.

"If someone really did break into my shop, then it must be connected to those two men," Elaina suggested.

"Maybe. I need to check the lock myself and have the sheriff dust for prints." He glanced down at his rumpled shirt. "I also need a change of clothes."

"Will Christopher and I stay here while you get your things?"

"Not a chance. You're coming with me." He took the oatmeal bowl from her hand. "I'll finish feeding Christopher while you get dressed."

Since she, too, wanted to get a look at that lock, she hurried into her bedroom and went to the closet. She reached for an ivory-colored sweater and jeans, and then turned back.

And that's when she noticed that her window was open, just a fraction.

She wasn't in the habit of leaving it open, but she wondered if Luke had done it while checking the security system. Elaina closed it and glanced around the room.

Something else wasn't right.

The box that'd contained the adoption papers. The night before she'd taken the box from the attic space above the closet and had put it on the corner desk. It was still there, but it'd been moved, practically to the edge.

She looked inside, at the meager files. Nothing seemed to be missing, but things were out of place. Specifically, the adoption papers with Kevin's signature. Elaina was certain she'd left them on top of the other files, but they'd been tucked inside.

With her clothes clutched in a death grip, Elaina returned to the kitchen. "Did you leave the window open or get anything from the box in my bedroom?"

"No to both." He stopped feeding Christopher and looked at her. "Why?"

"The files have been moved around."

Slowly, he stood. "As if someone had rummaged through them?"

Elaina nodded. "God, did Brenda do this? Or

maybe someone sneaked through the window and did it," she said, thinking out loud. "After all, the security system wasn't on while Carrie and Brenda were inside. Someone watching the house, like Gary for instance, might have known that."

But why would someone do this? Idle curiosity, maybe? After all, the box of papers had been just sitting there in plain sight. Maybe Brenda just wanted to see what they were. And maybe Gary had sneaked in because he was suspicious of Luke.

But Elaina couldn't be sure of that.

Obviously, neither could Luke.

He took out his phone. "I'll have a background check run on both. Within an hour, we should know who they really are and what one or both of them were really doing in your bedroom."

Chapter Eight

When Luke finished his call to headquarters, everything was official. He'd requested a full background check on Brenda McQueen and more extensive ones on Gary Simpson and Carrie Saunders. Hopefully, those checks would provide him with much needed answers to an ever-growing list of questions. He'd also informed his boss that he intended to work "this case" until everything was resolved.

His mind was racing, and he forced himself to slow down so he could think things through. He certainly hadn't counted on all these issues when he'd come up with the plan to get acquainted with his son.

First, there were the two now-jailed men. Once their lawyer showed up, he needed to figure out what part they had in all of this. Now, he could add Brenda to his list of persons of interest. He really didn't like the possibility that the woman or Carrie had rummaged through Elaina's files.

"You said that Brenda moved to Crystal Creek a few months ago?" Luke asked Elaina.

"Yes." She wiped the oatmeal from Christopher's face and took him from the high chair. "I think that's why we became friendly. Because we were both outsiders."

And maybe they'd become friends because Brenda had orchestrated it.

"Brenda's visited you here at the house before?" Luke wanted to know.

"Of course, but I don't think anything was out of place after she left." She kissed Christopher's hand when he patted her mouth and babbled Ma Ma. "But I can't be sure. I just wasn't looking for something like that."

Well, they'd be on the lookout for it now. If he let Brenda return, that is. Until he knew everything there was to know about her, Brenda wouldn't be making another visit.

The doorbell rang again, and like before, Luke reached for his gun. That reach put another look of near panic on Elaina's face, and he hated what all of this was doing to her. Thankfully, Christopher seemed oblivious to it. He continued to babble and make happy sounds.

Luke went to the door and looked out. He instantly relaxed. "It's Rusty."

Elaina blew out a long breath and probably because she still wore pj's, she took Christopher and headed for her bedroom. Luke disengaged the security system and greeted the one man he did want to see.

"Your suitcase," Rusty said, depositing the case inside the small foyer. He eyed Luke's rumpled clothes. "Hey, you really do look like a guy on his honeymoon."

Unfortunately, Luke felt that way sometimes, but he kept that to himself.

"What about the security equipment?" Luke asked, going straight for business. It'd lessen the chances of Rusty making any more honeymoon comments. Maybe it'd also lessen Luke's thoughts about such amorous activity.

"I have it with me. It shouldn't take me more than ten or fifteen minutes to install. Don't worry. I'll be discreet. I don't want Elaina's neighbors wondering what the heck I'm doing."

"Believe me, I appreciate that. Her neighbors and friends seem overly curious. One of them might have even rummaged through her things. I've already requested a background check," Luke added.

"Good. I guess it's too much to hope for a quick in and out for all of this."

Luke shook his head. "It doesn't look like it."

That brought on a few under-the-breath grumbles from Rusty. "I'll get that equipment installed. My advice? Take a shower. You look like you just climbed out of bed after several long rounds of really good sex."

Luke aimed some obligatory profanity at his fellow agent. "Wait right here a second. I want to give you Elaina's laptop so the lab can check it out. Her late fiancé might have left something about his illegal projects on it."

He left Rusty in the foyer while he went to Elaina's bedroom. The door was open just a fraction, and he fully opened it when he spotted Christopher sitting on the floor. His son was pounding the carpet with a small plastic hammer.

But Elaina was nowhere in sight.

Luke's reaction was immediate. A slam of adrenaline. His heart kicked into overdrive, and Luke raced across the room to see if she was in the adjoining bathroom. She wasn't.

He heard the movement in the closet and hurried there. Luke found her.

She was naked.

Well, practically naked, anyway. She wore just her underwear. Sheer pink panties and a matching bra. She quickly grabbed her robe to cover herself but not before he got an eyeful.

"I was dressing," she said. She sounded startled and out of breath.

Luke knew how she felt. He was having trouble breathing, too. Where the hell had the air gone? Better yet, where was his head? He obviously wasn't using it to think straight.

He finally looked away.

"I, um, needed to get your laptop. I didn't know you were changing. Sorry."

"No problem."

Oh, but it was a problem. A huge one. Despite all the crud going on around them, Luke didn't think he would be able to forget the sight of her in her pink panties.

He gave Christopher a quick kiss, and nearly got playfully bammed in the face with the plastic hammer. Luke grabbed the laptop from the desk, and took it to Rusty, who was still waiting for him by the front door.

"Let's hope we find something on this that we can use," Rusty commented. "And I'll call you if and when that lawyer shows up."

"Thanks."

Rusty turned to leave but then stopped. "Say, are you okay?"

"Why do you ask?" Luke countered, wondering just how poleaxed he really looked.

Rusty studied him a moment. "It's just that before you got to Crystal Creek, you were so riled that Elaina had taken your son."

Oh, that. Luke shrugged. "I don't think she had any part in the illegal adoption."

Rusty flexed his eyebrows. "Any reason for that change of heart?"

No logical one. "Gut instinct."

That caused Rusty to curse under his breath. "Elaina's a beautiful woman."

Luke stared. Nope, he glared. And hoped this wasn't going where he thought it might be going. "What the hell is that supposed to mean?"

Rusty aimed his index finger at him. "It means that you need to forget that she's beautiful. She loves that baby. We saw that when we had her under surveillance."

Luke's glare worsened. "And your point would be?"

Rusty's index finger landed against Luke's chest. "Elaina would do anything to keep your son. *Anything.* Just remember that."

Luke didn't need any help remembering that particular detail. He could say the same for the attraction he felt for her. And it was time to put an end to this finger-pointing visit. "Call me when that security equipment's installed," Luke grumbled, and he shut the door.

When he turned around, Elaina was standing there with Christopher in her arms. She was fully dressed, thank goodness. In addition to wearing an ivory-colored sweater and jeans, she was also wearing a scowl.

"I'm not faking this attraction," she volunteered. "In fact, I'm doing everything to nip it in the bud, understand? I wouldn't use sex to keep custody of Christopher."

He held up his hand in a mock act of surrender. "Rusty was wrong."

She made a yeah-right sound. "You suggested the same thing last night."

"And I was wrong." It was time to eat a little crow. All right, a *lot* of crow. "I was wrong about a lot of things. Your involvement, or lack thereof, in the adoption. About us being able to live together, pretending to be a loving couple, without it leaking into reality. We're both human. It's only natural to be attracted. Especially after seeing you in that pink underwear."

She looked ready to argue some more, but then the fight dimmed. Christopher might have had something to do with that. He began to kiss her cheek. It was difficult to stay angry with a cute kid showering you with sloppy kisses.

Elaina smiled at the baby's antics. Man, she glowed when she looked at Christopher. Luke stood there, watching them. And wanting to be part of it.

Well, he felt that way until Elaina looked at him.

"Is something wrong?" she asked.

"No." And he left it at that. "Rusty's in your backyard installing security equipment," he let her know. "I'd like to take a shower while he's in the area."

She combed her gaze over him. It took a while. She lingered on his unbuttoned shirt. "You can use my bathroom."

Luke's idiotic body wanted to watch her visual appraisal, but he forced himself to pick up his suitcase. Unfortunately, he felt uneasy with Elaina being out of earshot. Elaina likely felt the same.

That didn't mean she was going to like his suggestion.

"Considering what we just talked about, this is going to seem like a really dumb idea, but I need you to stay close to the bathroom while I'm showering," he insisted. "I want to be able to hear you if something goes wrong."

She nodded, picked up Christopher, and led him toward her bedroom. "I've been giving a lot of thought to things that could go wrong. I'm not anxious to experience whatever that might be. Not while Christopher is here, anyway. So, while watching you shower might be a little, uh, awkward, it's better than the alternative."

Luke couldn't agree more.

Elaina sank down onto the floor with Christopher. He immediately crawled out of her arms and lay belly first on the carpet. He jammed his right thumb into his mouth and began sucking it.

She pointed to her bathroom. "The shower curtain is opaque. And I won't peek."

For some reason, Luke found that amusing. "I peeked at your underwear," he pointed out because he thought they could use some levity.

It didn't have the effect Luke intended. Maybe it was the threat of danger or the intensity of the moment. Or maybe it was both. But Elaina didn't smile. Her mouth tightened, and she glanced away.

"You can leave the bathroom door open," she said, taking the plastic hammer from the baby. "And I can sit right here with Christopher."

Right here. In other words, very close to where he'd be naked and showering. Thankfully, his son would act as the ultimate chaperone. Nothing remotely sexual was going to happen with Christopher around.

Except Luke immediately had to rethink that when he looked down at his little boy.

Who had fallen asleep on the floor.

Oh, man.

So much for his chaperone.

Luke reached inside the shower stall, turned on the water and started to undress. His body apparently thought it was about to get lucky because he started to react in a totally male kind of way.

Frustrated with himself and this burning need for Elaina, he tossed his shirt into the sink. The jeans followed. Then his boxers. He turned to step into the shower, but the noise alerted him.

He turned around. Fast. A gut reaction to possible danger. But there was no danger. Well, not the ordinary kind anyway. There was just Elaina reaching for Christopher's plastic hammer that she'd apparently dropped on the floor beside her.

Elaina reacted, too. Her gaze flew in Luke's direction, probably so she could see what had caused his own reaction.

She froze.

Luke didn't exactly move, either. He just stood there. Naked. Elaina just sat there. Staring. And looking very interested in what she was seeing.

Chapter Nine

Elaina had several *oh-mercy* reactions at once. Luke had a hot body. A body so hot that it made her hot. But she was also aware that she shouldn't be looking at him and that she should be trying to hide what she suddenly wanted.

And what she suddenly wanted was Luke.

"The water will get cold," she mumbled, saying the first thing that came to mind. It was absurd because nothing had the potential to be cold in that room. Everything was sizzling.

Luke snared her gaze and waited a moment before he cursed and stepped into the shower.

Elaina didn't breathe a sigh of relief. She leaned her head against the doorframe and tried to stop the *sizzling* from getting any hotter.

Her body was acting insanely. She felt desperate and needy. Her, needy! She hadn't experienced those sensations in years. Which made her think about the whole crazy notion of attraction. It was making her feel like a hormone-crazed teenager. That had to stop. And she would make it stop, somehow.

Elaina's pep talk lasted mere seconds. She caught a glimpse of the outline of Luke's body behind that shower curtain. That obstruction was useless when up against her overly active imagination.

She could almost see him. Naked and wet. Heck, she could almost see herself in the shower with him. Doing things. Having shower sex.

What would it feel like to have him take her right then, right there?

Would he be gentle? No, she decided. Not with his intensity. But Elaina was positive that it would be one of the most pleasurable experiences of her life.

Elaina was imagining the pleasure of such a coupling when Luke's phone rang. Before going into the bathroom, he'd left it on her desk. Where he probably couldn't hear it. Since there was no way she was going to go tapping on that shower curtain, she answered the call.

"Hello," she said.

And she heard a long pause.

"This is Agent Rusty Kaplan. Is Luke there?"

Oh, Elaina really hated to say this. "He's in the shower."

Another pause. She could have sworn Agent Kaplan was filling in the blanks with naughty scenarios that involved Luke and her. But then, Elaina had done the same thing just seconds earlier.

"Get him please," Rusty insisted. "It's important."

Elaina glanced at the shower. Oh, mercy. The agent would want her to do that.

"Is this about Brenda McQueen?" she asked, making her way into the bathroom. She was certain that snails had moved faster than she was moving.

"Part of it is. I *really* need to talk to Luke."

Of course he did.

Turning her head, she tapped her fingers on the shower curtain. "You have a call from Agent Kaplan. He says it's important."

Maybe because she'd practically shouted, Luke turned off the water. Elaina grabbed a towel and had it ready for him when he pulled back the shower curtain. He tried to be discrete by using the curtain to cover himself.

It didn't work.

In fact, it made things worse.

Elaina got another glimpse that was only slightly concealed with the opaque vinyl material. She felt herself go warm and damp, and she knew that, coupled with the preshower incidents she had more than enough visual information about Luke to inspire a whole lot of fantasies.

He took the phone and the towel and managed to cover himself. But not before she got yet another glimpse of something she shouldn't be glimpsing at. Oh, mercy.

She had to fan herself.

With the water streaming down his body, he

stepped from the shower tub and onto the mat. "What's the problem, Rusty?" Luke asked.

Elaina watched his expression so she could try to gauge what the call was about, but there was no change in his demeanor. She started to step from the room, but Luke caught on to her arm. "I'll put the phone on speaker so Elaina can hear this."

"She's right there with you?" she heard Rusty ask the moment Luke pressed the speaker function.

"You said it was important," Elaina countered. "That's why I got him out of the shower."

"It *is* important," Rusty verified after pausing. "Don't trust Gary Simpson or Brenda McQueen. At least not until I can clear some things up. Let's start with Brenda. She's clean. Maybe a little too clean."

Elaina moved closer to the phone so she could hear him better. Unfortunately, that meant moving closer to Luke. He smelled good, and she hadn't remembered her soap smelling like that on her own skin.

"Brenda McQueen doesn't have a driver's license," Rusty continued. "No loans, no credit cards."

Elaina didn't have to ask if that was unusual. She knew it was. Heck, she was in hiding, living a lie and she still had a driver's license and credit card.

"You think Brenda assumed a fake identity or something?" Luke asked.

"Could be. Elaina might have a gut feel about this. Is she sort of recluse?"

"I guess you could say that. She doesn't get out much, and when she does, she either jogs or rides her bike. I remember her saying something about having a fear of cars because of a bad accident when she was a child."

"Dig deeper," Luke advised the other agent. "What about Gary Simpson?"

"One thing popped up. He recently had a rather large amount of money deposited into his bank account. I can't find a source for it."

"Maybe a payoff," Luke suggested.

"That's what I thought, too. He's certainly one to watch, especially since he's a former Army Ranger. He was discharged because he failed a personal reliability exam. In others words, he had some issues that made the army think he was no longer a suitable candidate to carry combat weapons."

Elaina knew none of that about Gary. Odd. Why wouldn't he have mentioned his military career, especially since he believed she had an MIA husband? Or maybe Gary hadn't bought her lie at all.

"See if you can access his military records," Luke continued. "And while you're at it, do a more thorough background on Carrie Saunders. It's possible one of them is working for a person known only as T. This T was involved with Elaina's ex-fiancé."

Well, that got her mind off his body. Luke actually suspected Carrie of something so devious? Elaina might be able to believe that about the other two, especially Gary, but not Carrie.

"The exterior security equipment is installed," Rusty continued. "It basically works like this. If anyone comes into the wooded area behind Elaina's house, then the motion detector will trigger a silent alarm, which will then send a signal to your cell phone. It'll sound as if you're getting a text message, and on your phone screen, you'll see the numbers 911. In this case, 911 means a trespasser."

"Thanks, Rusty. Let me know as soon as you have those background checks."

Luke ended the call and he placed his phone on the sink so he could give his towel a much needed adjustment. It was a little towel, and Luke was a big guy. Not a good combination. Well, not good unless she wanted another cheap thrill. She didn't.

Really.

Disgusted with herself, Elaina forced her snail-pace feet to get out of there. She went back into her room and sat on the edge of the bed. Luke closed the door, but not all the way, while he dressed. Unfortunately, she could see his reflection in the bathroom mirror.

Sheez. She didn't think her body could handle more of this, so Elaina forced herself to look away. She also forced her attention back on the issue at hand. And there was a huge issue at hand.

"Carrie isn't behind any of this," she informed him.

"*Everyone* is a suspect," Luke countered. "If T wants the software modifications badly enough, then he or she would have paid big bucks for someone to find them."

Elaina couldn't argue with that, but she could argue with the overall logic. "Then why wait until now? If it's Brenda, Gary or Carrie, why wouldn't they have started looking months ago?"

"Maybe they've been doing just that."

That sent a chill through her blood, but she couldn't completely discount it. Gary had been inside her house dozens of times, and she remembered that he'd used her bathroom once or twice. He'd also replaced a burned-out bulb when she'd mentioned that she didn't have a step ladder. Elaina hadn't stayed with him while he did it, and he could have easily gone through the things in her room. Or worse. With his training, he might have been able to sneak in while she wasn't even there.

"Okay, suppose one of them is our culprit," Elaina said. "Why step up the search now? Why risk rummaging through the house while both of us are here?"

"Maybe your security system prevented other searches when you were away from the house. And as for the timing, maybe that has something to do with me. The person could have gotten suspicious of my arrival. If he or she has some computer expertise, it wouldn't be that hard to figure out that I'm a federal agent."

Elaina gave that some thought and couldn't argue with it, either. "Especially if this person already knew that I didn't have a husband."

"You bet." He opened the door and faced her. Not naked this time. He wore jeans and black long-sleeve pullover. Both items of clothing hugged his body. "That means we need to find out who T is because he or she might do something stupid to get those modifications."

"Modifications I don't have," Elaina mumbled. But she wouldn't stand much of a chance of convincing T's hired guns of that. And then she thought of something else.

"What about this criminal you mentioned— George Devereux? The one you think had something to do with your wife's death. Do you still think he might have something to do with the two jailed men?"

"It's possible," Luke said. "I'd planned to visit Devereux tomorrow. He's in a federal prison not too far from here. But that visit's probably not going to happen. With any luck, I'll be doing the two interrogations at the local jail instead of seeing Devereux."

Yes, *that*. It suddenly seemed like too much to do, and all of it was important, if not critical. Elaina groaned and scrubbed her hands over her face. "So, we have Gary, Carrie, Brenda, George Devereux and heaven knows who else who might do something dangerous and crazy to get their hands on Kevin's final project?"

He lifted his shoulder. "And as you pointed out, it might not even be related to Kevin."

She'd known that, of course. But it was *not* knowing which was the truth that was getting to her.

"What I worry about most is Christopher," Elaina continued. "Greedy, desperate people often do greedy, desperate things, and I don't want there to be any possibility for Christopher to be hurt."

"Trust me." Luke eased down next to her on the bed. "I want the same thing."

"But how do we make sure it happens?" Her voice broke on the last word, and she thought for a moment that she might break, too. "There's so much coming at me. I'm not weak, I swear. But it scares me that I might not be able to protect him."

Her voice did more than break that time. It was a mess of quiver and nerves. Exactly the way she felt.

"My emotions are all over the place," Elaina admitted. "Like I have a nasty mix of ADD, PMS and adrenaline." She wouldn't mention the lustful urges, but they were there. It was like there was an alley-cat war going on inside her body.

Luke gave a heavy sigh. One with undertones of frustration and perhaps even disbelief at what he was about to do. He slipped his arm around Elaina and pulled her to him.

Elaina wanted to reject the gesture. She wanted to move away to regain her composure. But she didn't. She stayed put and took everything he was offering.

It felt like heaven.

It'd been so long since Elaina had relied on or trusted anyone other than herself. So long since she'd felt anything but lots of fear. But this wasn't fear. Luke was warm, solid, strong, and, if only for a few seconds, he made her believe that all was right with the world.

"I'm not weak," she repeated.

He chuckled. It was husky and low. Very manly. "You're not weak," he agreed. "Actually, you've handled this far better than most people would have."

Alarms went off in her head. Big ones. Elaina

pulled back and met Luke's gaze. "That sounds, um, friendly and compassionate."

He looked a little puzzled. "It was meant to be."

"Then, this isn't good." Elaina groaned.

"Probably not," he readily agreed. "This won't be a good idea, either."

"*This*?" she questioned.

He lowered his head. Slipped his hand around the back of her neck. And hauled her to him.

Luke kissed her.

His mouth was solid and warm, like the rest of him. That was her first thought. Her second, was that he was very good at this. He was at least a thirty on a scale of one to ten. He pressed his mouth against hers. Moving. Just a little. Touching the seam of her lips with his tongue. Again, just a little. But it was just enough to make her want so much more.

Giving into the need, Elaina lifted her arms, first one and then the other, and slid them around his neck. Her heartbeat slowed. Her breath became thin. Everything slowed, and the dreamy sensation of pleasure and heat washed over her. Like warm water on a tropical beach.

Luke pulled her closer to him. Until her breasts were against his chest. Until they seemed to be touching everywhere. Well, touching everywhere except in the place that wanted to be touched most. Elaina tried to push that urge aside so she could just concentrate on the pleasure of his mouth.

Long, slow French kisses. They were her passion.

And Luke was very good at satisfying that particular passion. He kissed and tasted, savoring her as she was savoring him.

Elaina knew she should stop. This wasn't a rocket science decision that required a lot of analysis. They were two aroused adults who shouldn't be aroused even after seeing each other practically naked. Yet, that logic didn't stop her when she slid her hand down his chest and had the pleasure of feeling all those muscles react and tense at her touch.

Luke touched, too. He never stopped the barrage of delicious kisses, but he escalated things in his own way. His hand left her neck, and he slid his fingers over her throat. Touching. Lighting little fires along the way.

His touch was weightless. Barely there. And yet, like his gentle kisses, it was enough. Thorough was the word that came to mind.

Luke was *thorough*.

The thoroughness went up a notch when those clever fingers made it to her breasts. He found her right nipple. It was puckered and tight from arousal and probably not hard to locate under her thin bra. He gently pinched her.

The hunger shot through her.

And the need. Mercy, the need. She could feel those stroking fingers on every part of her body. Here they were on her bed. Christopher was asleep. There was nothing to stop her from letting this lead to what would no doubt be the hottest sex she'd ever had.

But it couldn't happen.

Elaina repeated that to herself.

Her body tried to veto her decision, but she somehow managed to break the kiss. She had no idea that she had that much willpower, and after she looked at Luke, she wasn't sure that willpower would last more than a second or two.

"I didn't fake that kiss," she said, just to make sure he understood. And to make sure she could speak.

"I know." He leaned back slightly, and he reached out. He ran his thumb over her bottom lip, gathering up the moisture from their kiss. He then touched his thumb to his tongue and made a low sound of pleasure.

That simple gesture ignited her body again, and Elaina actually had to get up so that she wouldn't throw herself right back in his arms. Thankfully, she didn't have to put her failing willpower to the test because Luke's phone rang again. Not a normal ring. It was a series of beeps.

"You have a call," she said, forcing herself out of her lusty trance.

Even though her eyes were still blurry, she could see that he no longer had that look of lust. "It's not a call," he let her know. "That's a text message."

Luke hurried off the bed and picked up his phone from her dresser. He cursed when he glanced at the screen. "Someone or something tripped the exterior security system."

Elaina couldn't say anything. Before that mind-numbing kiss, she'd just been thinking of the danger.

And now, it might be here. Not some vague sense of unease. The danger might be right outside her door.

Luke took something from his suitcase that was still sitting on the bathroom floor. It was a small black gun. He removed what appeared to be a safety lock from it, and he pressed it into her hands.

"Wait here with Christopher," he instructed.

She didn't want to wait. She didn't want to move, either. And she definitely didn't want to panic. But that's what she seemed to be on the verge of doing.

Elaina forced herself to breathe and spring into action. She got down on the floor to shelter Christopher's body, and she prayed that the security equipment had malfunctioned. Maybe that was all there was to it. But her out-of-control heart and mind were screaming differently.

Moments later, she heard Luke's hurried footsteps in the hall. "There's a fire out back."

"A fire?" A dozen things went through her mind, and none of them were good.

"I've already called the fire department," Luke told her. "Lock this door and stay inside."

Her out-of-control feeling soared. "You're going out there?" she asked, instantly alarmed.

"I have to. I need to use the hose to try to put out the fire, or the flames might make it to the house."

Oh, God. Now, she was ready to panic. "My house might burn down?"

"Not if I can stop it. If the fire gets out of hand, you'll hear me shout for you to take the baby and evacuate. Don't leave unless you hear me say differently. Try not to worry. This could be nothing."

One brief glance passed between them, and in that glance, she could tell that Luke was trying to reassure her before he rushed away. She heard the back door close, and she heard the clicks to indicate he'd locked it. Elaina got up, as well, and went to the window. She didn't open the blinds, but she peeked out.

There was black smoke billowing from the woods.

The fire wasn't close, at least twenty yards away, but it was close enough for Elaina to catch a whiff of the smoke and feel the horrible threat that seemed to be closing in around her house. Worse, the ground was winter dry, and there was a cold wind blowing. That fire could easily get out of control.

She saw Luke. He had his gun in one hand, and the hose in the other. He was spraying the water on the fire. Unfortunately, the flames were large, and the water pressure wasn't any match for them.

Elaina wanted to run out and help him, but one glance at Christopher, and she knew she couldn't. She couldn't leave her baby alone. So, she waited with her heart in her throat, and with her concerns and questions growing.

She put a halt to some of those concerns by reminding herself that all of this could have been an accident. This could have been caused by a spark from Gary's barbecue grill. It didn't matter that it was still morning and in the dead of winter. Elaina had seen him using that grill at all times of the day and in all kinds of weather.

And then she heard a sound.

It was something coming not from the fire area but from the front of the house. It sounded as if someone were testing the doorknob.

Oh, mercy.

Elaina hadn't thought things could get worse, but she was obviously wrong.

She glanced at the gun and hoped she could shoot straight. Since she'd never tried, she doubted she could, but the gun made her feel marginally safer.

The doorknob jiggled again.

She tried not to make a sound because she didn't want to give away her position in the house, but she tiptoed to her bedroom door and unlocked it. She stepped into the hall. This time, Elaina didn't just hear the knob move, she saw it.

The motion was almost frantic as if someone were desperately trying to pick the lock. Which in all likelihood, that's exactly what was happening.

She couldn't go to the door and look out the peephole. Too risky. This person might have a gun, as well. Worse, the person might know how to use it. Unlike her. But she couldn't just stand there and let someone break in, either. She couldn't risk Christopher being hurt.

"Get away from the door now, or I'll shoot," Elaina shouted.

The jiggling immediately stopped.

She heard footsteps, and she wanted to run and see who was responsible for them, but again, she raced back to Christopher in case the intruder tried to come through a window or another door.

Then, a terrifying thought hit her.

What if this would-be intruder went after Luke? Oh, God. What if something happened to him?

Elaina had never felt more helpless in her life. She couldn't leave the house, and she had no way to help him. So, she stood there, her hands aching from the grip she had on the gun.

More seconds ticked off the clock. It seemed to take an eternity, but Elaina finally heard something that she wanted to hear.

The siren.

That meant the fire engine was approaching her house. She hurried to the blinds and looked out. It wasn't long before she saw the two firemen running across her lawn.

She said a quick prayer of thanks, but that prayer got a lot longer when she heard the key in the back door. She waited, just in case, but then she heard the security system being reengaged.

It was Luke.

Elaina raced out into the hall and saw him in the kitchen.

"Are you okay?" She couldn't help herself. Elaina ran into his arms and held on tight.

"I'm fine." He sounded out of breath, and he

smelled of the scorched wood and smoke. There were smears of black ash on his face and clothes.

Elaina wasn't sure she believed him. "Someone tried to get in through the front door. I was afraid he'd go after you."

Alarmed, Luke shook his head. "No one came after me."

"Thank God." She brushed some soot off his chin. "What about the fire?"

"It should be out in no time. The house isn't in danger."

That was good news, but there wasn't happiness in his eyes. He eased back and looked down at her.

"I smelled accelerant while I was out there," he whispered. "I'm almost certain it was gasoline."

Elaina held her breath and waited for him to finish what she already knew he was going to say.

"Someone intentionally set that fire. It was arson."

Chapter Ten

Luke was mad as hell.

He didn't like the speed with which things were moving. He didn't like the evidence, or lack there-of, in what was now officially an arson investiga-tion. And he didn't like feeling as if he were spinning his wheels at one of the most crucial times in his life.

"We have the car packed and ready to go. What do you mean the safe house isn't ready yet?" Luke demanded. He made that demand of the agent in San Antonio who was handling his request. A delay wasn't an option, not after dealing with that fire.

Luke had to get Elaina and Christopher some place safe.

"We're working as fast as we can," the agent on the other end of the line insisted.

"Then, work faster." Luke stabbed the End Call button and got up to pace. It didn't help. But then, not much would help at this point. Well, not much other than a call to say the safe house was ready and that the arsonist had been caught and was behind bars.

"It's already getting dark," Elaina commented. She was in the kitchen feeding Christopher dinner. Mushy peas and some other food item that Luke couldn't readily identify. It looked disgusting, but Christopher was wolfing it down. "Does that mean we'll stay the night here?"

"No. Absolutely not." He softened his tone when he heard the harshness. "The safe house will be ready soon."

"And then what?" she asked.

It wasn't an easy question for him to answer. "Once I have Christopher and you settled in, and once I'm sure that you'll be okay there, then I need to find out who's playing these games."

"You think the fire was a *game?*"

"More like a ruse. I think the arsonist wanted us out of the house and was willing to create a diversionary tactic to make that happen."

Elaina gave that some thought. "The arsonist did this so he or she could get inside and search while we were out there battling flames."

Luke nodded. "I think that was the plan. But this idiot obviously didn't realize that there was no way I would let you outside like that with Christopher."

"True. But Rusty said there weren't any useable prints on the doorknob. Only smears." She met his gaze. There was so much weariness in her eyes. "So, maybe this person isn't as stupid as we'd like to believe he or she is. Maybe he or she wiped down the knob. Or wore gloves."

"Could have. But anyone who's ever watched a crime show would have done that. What it does tell me is that this person is under some kind of pressure to come up with something—*fast*. Probably those modifications to Kevin's software."

"Or it could be the adoption papers," she offered cautiously.

Luke couldn't rule that out. And if it was the papers that had precipitated it, then this was his fault. He'd literally brought this right to Elaina's door. Either way, no matter what this person wanted, Luke would have to find a way to stop him or her.

He had his list of suspects, and while technically anyone in town could be guilty, his primary ones included: Carrie, Brenda, Gary and his old nemesis, George Devereux. Carrie was least suspect of those four, but Luke wasn't about to take her off the list. He'd learned the hard way that people would do all sorts of things for money. Besides, Carrie had had just as much opportunity to set that fire as Brenda and Gary. Devereux was the unknown factor here.

And Luke was soon going to remedy that.

Elaina took Christopher out of the high chair. "So, we go to the safe house, what will happen then?"

She eyed him suspiciously. It made Luke wonder if he was that transparent or if she'd managed to figure him out. Odd, because most people accused him of being hard to read. That kiss had probably broken down some barriers and created an intimacy and familiarity that shouldn't exist between them. Those kinds of connections could cause him to lose focus. That couldn't happen.

"There'll be an agent at the safe house," Luke explained after he cleared his throat. "Someone I trust. He'll stay with you and Christopher."

"And where will you be?" Judging from her expression, she'd already guessed the answer.

"Here."

Yep. Elaina had guessed, and she wasn't happy about it. *"Here?"*

"I need to search the place, and I can't do that if I'm worried about Christopher." He almost added Elaina's name in there, because he would worry about her, too, but it was best not to add any more of that familiarity to this already dangerous mix.

She shifted Christopher to her hip, and both of them gave him an accusing stare. "So, you're going to put yourself in danger and possibly make yourself a target?"

That about summed it up. "I'm a federal agent, Elaina. This is what I do. Besides, I wouldn't be any more of a target than I am right now."

She didn't say anything for several moments. "Maybe," Elaina finally mumbled.

He knew what she was thinking and what terrified her. He also knew that her semicalmness was a façade. "Christopher and you are targets, too." And it was hard as hell to admit the rest it aloud. "You can blame me for that."

Her gaze whipped to his. Elaina stared at him. But she didn't deny it. She couldn't.

When she rubbed her fingers over her forehead, he noticed she was trembling. The façade was crumbling fast. "Sometimes I just want to run and hide again." Her voice was trembling, too. "I want Christopher to be safe."

Luke wanted that, as well. It hurt to know that he couldn't make that promise.

He reached for her, but Elaina moved away. She sank down onto the sofa and placed Christopher on the floor so he could play with his toys. "I'm scared," she admitted.

Those two words encompassed a lot. Elaina was scared of this arsonist-intruder who'd come into her life. She was scared of another attack. Scared of her uncertain future. But that wasn't all.

"You're scared of *me*," Luke said. He sat down in the chair directly across from her.

When she lifter her head and met his gaze, he could see that Elaina was blinking back tears. She stared at him. Then, she nodded. "I *am* scared of you."

Even though he'd braced himself, it was still difficult to hear. "Your fears are justified."

She shook her head. "I don't want to make the same mistakes I made with Kevin—"

"I'm not Kevin."

"I know." Every part of her was filled with emotion. Her voice. Her body. Her eyes. "But I've let that kiss and my feelings for you get in the way. I can't see you objectively. I can't see myself objectively. And things are moving so fast. That can't be good because I have to think beyond this day and this week. I have to look at the future, and I have to wonder where we'll be if and when this attraction fizzles out."

Luke knew exactly how she felt. In less than two days, he'd gone from despising Elaina to kissing her.

And worse, he wanted to kiss her again.

So that he wouldn't do just that, he got up and moved away from her. Elaina took the cue. She picked up Christopher and headed for her bedroom. Luke followed them because he didn't want her to be anywhere in the house without him.

He wanted to do something to ease her fear, but the only thing that would accomplish that would be to identify the person after them. So, that's the direction Luke took.

"I have an idea," he said. "Why don't you get out everything else you brought with you from San Antonio? Clothes, toys, everything. I have to go through all of that anyway, and this way, it'll save some time."

As if it were the most natural thing in the world, she handed Christopher to him. His son went willingly and didn't give Luke that disapproving look that he sometimes did. In fact, Christopher snuggled against him and gave him a sloppy kiss on the cheek.

The whole situation suddenly seemed so intimate. They seemed like a family. But they weren't. Still, that didn't stop Luke from playing what-if.

Could he possibly make this work with Elaina?

He quickly came to his senses and decided he didn't want to know. It wasn't the right time to try to work through all of this. Truth was, it might never be the right time. Elaina could be correct—this attraction could all fizzle out and leave them both with bad tastes in their mouths.

Which made him think of her mouth, again.

He was in danger of developing a case of obsession.

"I had on these clothes the day I left." She deposited a pair of dark gray pants, a top in a lighter shade and a pair of shoes. Another reach into the closet, and she added a purse to the pile. It was empty, Luke soon learned, after Christopher and he had a look inside. Christopher didn't stop with a look, he began to slap at the purse and laugh. He even tried to put it on his head.

Luke smiled and kissed him.

Despite the wonderful moment, Luke knew he should be concentrating. His precious son was yet another distraction. The sooner he had him in a safe house, the better.

Elaina put the box of files on the bed, and then she went into the nursery. When she returned she had several items in her hands. "These are the toys I brought with me." She put those next to the other things.

There were two small stuffed animals. A purple

bear and a yellow bunny that drew Christopher's attention. He ditched the purse for it.

"Kevin had these with him the night he brought Christopher home," Elaina explained. "He called Christopher our little bunny."

Luke didn't care much for a criminal giving his son a pet name. "This is everything?" he asked.

She shook her head. "I honestly don't know. There could be other things."

Luke was afraid she'd say that. "When you get to the safe house, sit down and write a list. That way, I know what to look for when I come back."

"Suit yourself, but it'd be easier if I just went through everything in person."

"It wouldn't be *safer*," he reminded her. That earned him an eye roll. "You said Kevin used a miniature memory card. So, we're looking for something very small, just as thin as a dime."

"Something Kevin might have had on him the night he was killed," Elaina pointed out.

"No. If it'd been on him, then someone wouldn't still be looking for it. They would have found it. I read the police report of Kevin's death, and he'd been stripped and searched—thoroughly. So had his car."

Luke sat on the bed so he could better examine all the items. The most obvious things were the purse and toys. He squeezed all three and looked closely at the small details. The bunny's glassy eyes. The bear's padded black nose. The strap of Elaina's purse. There were no obvious signs of the memory card, but these things needed to be checked and double-checked.

"I'm going to put this stuff in the car," he let her know, passing Christopher back to her. "I can take it to my office in San Antonio once you're settled into the safe house."

Elaina opened her mouth, probably to argue about him returning here, but his cell phone rang. Finally! That safe house had to be ready. But the person who spoke to him on the other end of the line wasn't from the Justice Department.

"Luke, it's Collena Drake," the woman greeted.

He certainly hadn't expected to hear her voice, and it brought back a barrage of memories. The search for his son. The frustration of not being able to find him. And then, Collena's help. If it hadn't been for her, he'd no doubt still be looking for Christopher. Luke owed her a lot that he'd never be able to repay.

"I had to call," Collena continued, her voice rusty and thick as if laced with too much emotion and fatigue. "Did you connect with your son?"

"I found him, yes. I can't thank you enough."

"You don't have to thank me. In fact, it's my guess that the adoptive mother would want to do the opposite. If she's a good loving mother, then having you learn the truth must have turned her world upside-down."

"It has." Luke wasn't immune to the guilt he was feeling over that, either.

"Well, it might take time, but you'll work through this. I'm sorry it took so long to get you the information to find your son. The files were a mess. Little bits of info in one place. Other bits in other places. It took time to put the pieces together."

That opened the door for something that Luke had wanted to ask from day one. "Why did you help me?"

She chuckled. It was rusty like her voice. "Penance, of sorts."

"Yours or mine?"

"Mostly mine. I was the undercover cop investigating the Brighton Birthing Center. If I'd been able to identify the culprits sooner, then some of those babies would have never been illegally adopted."

There was no mistaking the pain in that. "Something tells me you paid hard for that."

"I have. I'm still paying," she added in a mumble. "I found something else in the files, and I thought you should know. First of all, the leaders of the adoption ring have all been arrested. The police are now in the process of rounding up the investors."

"There were investors?" This was the first Luke had heard of it.

"Lots of them. I don't believe that most knew they were providing funds for illegal activities. And in some cases, the activities weren't illegal at all. Which brings me to the point of this call. Before I gave you the information about how to find your son's adoptive mother, I checked your background. I wanted to make sure you were a suitable father."

Luke wasn't surprised by that. He'd checked her background, too. "And what did you find?"

"You're suitable. But I also learned that you're the one responsible for putting George Devereux behind bars."

Luke's stomach knotted. He did not like hearing that connection. "Didn't you have a minor role in that, too? You were on one of the surveillance teams when you were still with San Antonio PD. It's a small world." He paused. "Some things have been happening here. A suspicious fire. And someone might have rummaged through Elaina's bedroom. Do you think Devereux could be behind what's going on here?"

"I don't know. But I've learned that he's connected to the Brighton Birthing Center where your son was born. Luke, George Devereux was one of their investors."

Chapter Eleven

Elaina had to sit back down on the bed after hearing what Collena Drake had just told Luke.

Mercy.

She didn't want a man like Devereux involved in this. Now, the question was—how involved was he? Being an investor in a birthing center didn't mean he had a hand in Taylor's death or Christopher's adoption. It also didn't mean he had a part in what was happening now.

But then, it didn't mean he was innocent, either.

Luke obviously felt the same because the moment he finished giving her the news, he began to make phone calls. The first was to Rusty to brief him on what Collena Drake had told him. The second call was to the Justice Department office in San Antonio. With both calls, he requested the status of the safe house and a thorough check on Devereux's recent activities.

However, that wasn't all.

Elaina listened as he made some comments laced with frustration and anger. Then he set up an appointment with Devereux for the following day.

"You think meeting with George Devereux is a wise thing to do?" she asked the moment Luke finished the call and put his phone into his pocket.

Christopher fussed, and she picked him up from the floor. Elaina rocked him gently to soothe him. She only wished it had a soothing effect on her, but that wasn't going to happen. Not with Luke less than twenty-four hours from meeting with a convicted felon.

"I have to find out if Devereux is part of this," Luke answered.

"I understand that. But what if the meeting only upsets him even more? What if seeing you makes him want to come after you?"

"It's a risk I have to take. I won't meet with him until Christopher and you are in the safe house. So, if Devereux wants to retaliate against anyone, then I'll be the only one he can come after."

Elaina couldn't believe what she'd just heard him say. "Well, that's just great. He'll come after you and only you. Is that supposed to make me feel better?" She couldn't sit still any longer. She stood and began to rock back and forth. Christopher must have liked the motion because he put his head on her shoulder, and she felt him relax.

"You're angry."

"You're right." But then, she heard herself and groaned softly.

"See, this is the problem with having feelings for someone," he concluded. "Now, instead of thinking of the best way to approach this case, you're thinking about the possibility that I might be in danger."

Since that was dead-on accurate, she didn't bother to respond.

"I'm dealing with the same thing," he admitted. "What I should do is turn all of this over to another agent. One who isn't personally involved. That's by-the-book." He put his hands on his hips. "But I can't do that, and that means this isn't fair to you or Christopher."

"It's fair," she insisted.

He walked closer, and he lightly touched Christopher's back. "He's asleep."

That didn't surprise her. He'd had a very short afternoon nap, so she wasn't going to wake him even if she hadn't had a chance to bathe him yet. Elaina took him into the nursery and put him in the bed.

Luke followed her, of course, and stood in the doorway waiting.

"I'll get him up when it's time to leave for the safe house," she whispered.

He got that concerned look again. Luke reached out, touched her arm, and rubbed softly. It was soothing, or at least it would have been if she hadn't been waiting to hear what would no doubt be bad news.

"The safe house probably isn't going to be ready tonight," Luke confessed.

That didn't do a thing to steady Elaina's raw

nerves. "Well, that explains why you got so angry while you were on the phone."

"Anger is too mild a word for what I was feeling when I found out." Luke took a deep breath. "We're going to plan B. Just for tonight, we'll stay here, and Rusty will sit outside in his car and make sure no one gets near the place."

It wasn't ideal, but then nothing about this situation was. She could only hope that the culprit wasn't stupid enough to return with a federal agent standing guard. Plus, they had the security systems to give them warning if someone did try to approach the house or break in.

"I don't want you to turn this case over to another agent," Elaina told him. "This will probably sound maudlin, but you would do everything possible to protect Christopher. I can't say the same about another agent, and that's too big of a risk to take."

He stared down at her, and Elaina could have sworn he was fighting a smile. It didn't last long before the concern returned. "I don't have a good track record when it comes to a personal life."

Now, she fought a smile. It seemed an odd change of subject. "Is that meant to be some kind of warning?"

"Yeah," he readily admitted.

She shrugged. "You don't have to be good at it, Luke. Not when it comes to us. Just a few minutes ago, we admitted that this isn't personal." That hadn't sounded as good as it had while still in her head. "What I mean is that it's simply an attraction between two adults who haven't had sex in a long time." She winced. That didn't sound right, either. "Well, that's true in my case."

"My case, too. For months I've been obsessed with finding Christopher. That hasn't given me much time for anything else."

"So." And she wasn't sure what to add to that. Maybe she could say something along the lines of *there, we've established an out for us, again.*

But it was beginning to feel like a situation where the lady doth protest too much.

He was close enough for her to touch him. Close enough to see the swirls of gray in his eyes. Close enough to feel his breath brush against her face. It stirred her blood. Stirred her body.

And the heat rolled through her.

His touch didn't help things, either. He slid his fingers along the outside of her arm. A sensual, slow caress.

"Talking about sex probably isn't a good idea," he commented.

But he didn't move.

"Just remember all the anger you feel toward me." She didn't move, either.

"The anger," he repeated. He nodded. Nodded again. And for a moment, she really thought that was going to do the trick. Elaina expected him to back away. To put up those shields and barriers that were in both of their arsenals of relationship avoidance.

He didn't.

Luke latched on to her hair with one hand, the back of her neck with the other, and he hauled her to him.

LUKE DIDN'T EVEN try to hold anything back. He would have failed anyway. He knew it. His body knew it. And his brain just surrendered to the inevitable.

Elaina surrendered, too.

She melted against him, and she let him take her mouth as if he owned her. Ironic, because even with the heat and the need slamming through him, he knew that she was not his for the taking. This was temporary. A lull before the storm of a custody battle. He'd deal with that when the time came. For now, he intended to take everything she was offering, even if it was a really bad idea.

Luke maneuvered her so that her back was against the wall and kissed her, deeper and harder. The kiss didn't stop, it escalated. Elaina's mouth was suddenly just as hungry, just as demanding as his. Not a good combination for a couple who had any hopes of trying to maintain a hold on their feelings.

She came up on her tiptoes and coiled her arms around him. Luke reacted to the intimate contact. Man, did he ever react. He pressed his body against hers. Tightly against her. Until they were perfectly aligned. His chest against her breasts. The front of her pants against his jeans.

Elaina reacted, too.

She made a throaty moan of pleasure and

deepened the kiss. The taste of her fired through him, as did the feel of her in his arms. She fit. *They* fit. A thought that had him doing a mental double take.

Luke might have stepped away from her to consider why he shouldn't be thinking that way, but their midsections brushed against each other. Specifically, her soft feminine body brushed against his erection. And all doubts and coherent thoughts went straight out the window.

The kissing session became a different kind of battle—they fought to get closer to each other. They fought for the intimate contact. The connection of man and woman. Each touch, each brush of her hips fanned the flames higher, and Luke knew he was lost.

She slid her leg along the outside of his, creating even deeper contact between them. Luke let go of her hair so he could shove up her stretchy top. Thankfully, the top cooperated, and he suddenly had her bra-covered breast in his hand. He shoved down the bra, as well, though it was hardly more than a swatch of lace, and she spilled into his hand.

He broke the kiss long enough to go down her body and take her nipple into his mouth. She moaned with desire. And she grabbed on to him and pulled him closer.

Luke didn't stop there. He kissed her stomach, circling her navel with his tongue, and he sucked her. Not gently, either.

She said something. Something incoherent because his pulse was pounding in his ears. Elaina didn't need words, however, to make herself clear. She slid down, as well, and eased her palm over his erection.

Luke damn near lost his breath.

The sensation was so intense that he knew this couldn't last long. He considered carrying her to the bed. Or maybe the floor. Taking her. In some hard, fast, frantic coupling that would exhaust this maddening need for release.

But he also knew this was definitely not the time for full-blown sex.

After all, his sleeping son was only a few yards away from them. And if they had sex, he certainly wouldn't be thinking about protecting Christopher and Elaina. His brainless body would take over, and he'd only one thought on his mind. *Take Elaina now.*

She obviously had the same thought in her mind, too, because she tried to unzip his jeans. Luke put his hand over hers to stop her. He had to distract her before she made a second attempt because he didn't think he could resist her if she got his zipper down.

Luke shoved his hand down her stomach, past her pants, and into her panties. His fingers found her. Wet and hot. He made his way through the slick moisture. A few strokes, and she gave up the zipper quest.

One touch, and he heard her breath break.

She slid her hand into her own hair, her eyelids fluttered down, and she rocked against his fingers. He could feel her already so close to release, and he took her mouth so he could taste her when she shattered.

But Elaina obviously had something else in mind.

While he was distracted, she went in for the kill. She was fast, too. Damn fast. One deft move, and she had his zipper down, and her hand was inside his jeans.

She didn't fumble or hesitate. Those agile fingers bypassed his boxers and slid right over his erection. She proved that she was just as adept at stroking and touching as he was. A rather skillful swipe of her thumb, and she had him close to begging for the sex that he already knew they couldn't have.

It became a war of will, and Luke fell back on his combat training. He couldn't lose concentration because it would simply be too dangerous.

On many levels.

Including a personal one.

Luke gritted his teeth and dragged her to the carpeted floor. He landed on her. Between her legs. All in all, it wasn't a bad place to be. For a moment, anyway. But he had to gain even more control of the situation. He caught both her hands in one of his. Imprisoning her.

It worked…for a few seconds.

And then there was another round of jockeying for position. She didn't have use of her hands, but she made use of her body. She lifted her hips, thrust them forward, and the friction nearly caused them both to shatter.

The second phase of the battle began. He wedged his knee between her legs and eased his fingers back inside her. Just like that, Elaina stopped struggling. Thank goodness. She gave into the moment.

Luke practically cheered. This was a battle he couldn't lose. Somehow, someway, he had to keep his wits and sanity, even if it required multiple cold showers later.

A long, deliberate sigh left her mouth. Once again she moved into the strokes. And she moved against him. Deeper this time. Against his fingers, against his body. A slow, sensual slide that brought out every basic, every carnal instinct inside him.

"We can do this," Elaina whispered, her voice threaded with the heat. "Together." But it was the passion talking. Later, she'd thank him for holding back.

Even if he wouldn't be thanking himself.

"I don't have a condom," Luke lied. "We'll have to do it this way."

He snagged her gaze, because he wanted to see her face. Luke fought through the clawing primal need to claim and possess so he could see exactly what this did to her. Elaina shook her head, as if she wanted to pull back, as if she wanted to wait for him.

But Luke deepened the strokes inside her. He kissed her, hard. He added some pressure with the leg still wedged between hers. He touched and touched and kept on touching until she no longer shook her head. Until she couldn't catch her breath. Elaina could only do one thing.

Surrender.

He felt her go over. Tasted her mouth as the pleasure rushed through her body. And when she melted, he gathered her into his arms and held her.

Elaina's eyes stayed closed for several seconds. Her body stayed limp. Then, she opened her eyes and looked at him. She looked on the verge of saying something—what exactly, he didn't have a clue. But whatever was on her mind, she didn't have a chance to tell him.

His phone beeped.

That soft little sound tore through his body like a bullet.

"Text message," he managed to say. Hoping he wouldn't see the numbers on the screen, he pulled his phone from his pocket and looked down.

The numbers were there. Nine-one-one.

"Someone tripped the security equipment out back," he told Elaina.

He didn't watch her reaction, but he didn't have to do that to know it wouldn't be good. She quickly got to her feet and fixed her clothes.

Luke did the same, and he called Rusty. It took him two rings to answer, and with each ring, Luke's adrenaline skyrocketed. "We might have an intruder in the backyard," he relayed when Rusty finally answered. "The security equipment just went off."

"I don't see anything out there. Stay put. I'll have a look around."

"Be careful."

Luke ended the call and waited. While Elaina stood directly across from him. She smelled like sex. Looked like it, too. But his brain had already kicked into protection mode. He reached over and turned off the overhead light in the nursery.

"Deer sometimes feed out there at night," she said. There was no more heat and passion in her voice. Only concern.

He nodded. Prayed that's all there was to it. And waited some more. He stared down at the screen, willing Rusty to phone back with a good report.

That didn't happen.

There was a crash. The sound of breaking glass. And it came from the nursery.

Because Luke knew what it was, he automatically pulled Elaina back to the floor. But he didn't stop there. He scrambled toward the crib in the nursery so he could get Christopher.

Christopher was alone, thank God. His son woke up and started to fuss. Luke ignored him and dropped with him to the floor. He sheltered Christopher with his body so the baby wouldn't be hurt. Then, Luke started the mad scramble back to Elaina's bedroom so he could turn off the light there and get his gun.

"We have an intruder," Elaina said. She sounded terrified. And no doubt was.

Luke knew what he was about to tell her would terrify her even more.

"That wasn't an intruder. That was a gun rigged with a silencer. Someone just fired a shot into the house."

Chapter Twelve

Elaina took Christopher from Luke so that he could grab his gun from her dresser. Within the span of a few seconds, she'd gone from postorgasmic bliss to sheer terror.

Someone had fired a shot into the house.

A shot that could have hurt Christopher.

There was another crash of glass, and Elaina knew another round had been fired.

But where?

The first had obviously been fired into the nursery, but this one appeared to have come from the direction of the living room. In other words, the front of the house. The gunman wasn't standing still.

He was on the move.

Or there was more than one.

With the overhead lights off, she had to rely on the meager light filtering into the hall from the kitchen. It was literally the only interior light still left on. She checked the baby for any signs of an injury, but he was fine. Well, except for the fact that he was crying at the top of his lungs. Christopher had no doubt been startled when Luke pulled him from the crib. But thank God Luke had reacted so quickly. Elaina didn't want to think about what might have happened if Luke hadn't done what he did.

"Stay on the floor," Luke ordered.

Elaina did, and she sheltered Christopher with her own body. She tried to soothe him by humming, but she failed miserably. But then, Christopher could likely feel the fear and concern in her.

Luke crawled forward so that he was between her and the door so he could fire if someone stormed into the house and tried to get into the bedroom.

"Press redial," he said passing his cell phone to her. "Ask Rusty what the hell is going on out there."

Somehow, she managed to do that, though she had to struggle with Christopher who was trying to wiggle out of her arms. "Someone fired a bullet into the house," she relayed to Rusty the moment he answered.

Silence.

Even over Christopher's sobs, Elaina could hear breathing so she knew someone was there on the other end of the line. God, was he hurt, unable to speak?

Or had something much worse happened?

And if so, if Rusty had been killed or incapacitated, then who was this on the phone?

Elaina snared Luke's gaze and passed the phone to him. He pressed the phone to his ear, listened.

Waited. "Agent Foley, if you can hear me, we're inside, in the kitchen. Can you get to us?"

"Did he answer?" Elaina mouthed.

Luke shook his head. He listened several more seconds and then ended the call.

Since Luke had obviously lied to the caller, that meant he probably didn't think this was his fellow agent.

Did that mean that Rusty was dead?

Who was this SOB who'd put her son in danger? She only wished she could get her hands around his throat.

Thinking of the danger reminded her that someone might be lurking around the house. So, he would know where to fire the next shot. Christopher's crying would make them much easier to find. It could make them targets.

Elaina tried again to soothe the baby. She kissed him, forced herself to hum a lullaby and she began to move in a rocking motion. Thankfully, Christopher cooperated, and his sobs tapered off to soft whimpers. He finally hushed, and Elaina prayed that he'd gone back to sleep. She didn't want him to have to experience any of this.

Luke jabbed in more numbers on his phone. "Sheriff Dawson," she heard him say. "This is Elaina's husband. Someone is firing shots into the house. Agent Foley is somewhere on the grounds, but he's not responding. We need assistance immediately."

But how soon would that be? Elaina calculated the distance between the sheriff's office and her house.

With luck, he could be there in five minutes if he came alone. Ten minutes, if he waited for backup from the deputy. That wasn't an eternity, but she was certain it would feel that way before this was over.

With his gun aimed and ready, Luke stayed in a crouching position and made his way to the hall. He looked out and lifted his head, listening. Elaina listened, as well, but she didn't hear anything.

That thought had no sooner formed in her mind, when there was another crash.

From the kitchen.

"Stay put," Luke whispered. "Keep Christopher quiet if you can."

Alarmed, Elaina frantically shook her head. "What are you going to do?"

"Create a diversion."

Elaina definitely didn't like the sound of that, but then she didn't care much for the crash of more breaking glass. It was still coming from the kitchen. Why hadn't the security alarm gone off? Someone must have disarmed it.

Luke backtracked toward her and dragged the mattress from her bed. He shoved it in front of the window and then hurried back to the hall.

"Be careful," Elaina whispered, but she said it so softly that she doubted he heard her.

A few seconds later, the light came on in the nursery. She craned her neck and saw Luke crouched down just outside the nursery door. He was waiting for another round bullet, probably so he could return fire.

Christopher stirred, and she began to hum to him again. Her breath was all over the place, and she wasn't sure she could produce enough sound to keep Christopher quiet. But her lullaby was interrupted by another crash.

Another bullet.

This one in the nursery again. So, the gunman was watching for any sign of activity and had fallen for Luke's diversion. Elaina only prayed that the shots stayed in the room and didn't stray into the hall where Luke was. He'd put himself in the line of fire to save them. She hadn't doubted he would do that, but that didn't stop her fears from soaring.

Luke couldn't be hurt.

He had to stay safe.

She didn't care if she felt that way because of what had happened earlier in the hall. She didn't care if lust and attraction were part of this. Elaina just wanted the shots to stop and for Christopher, Luke and her to be unharmed.

There was a slash of light in the front of the house. She thought of the earlier fire, but there weren't any flames. She heard the slam of a car door, and hoped that signaled the arrival of the sheriff.

There were more shots.

All the bullets came spewing through the nursery windows. One right after another. She counted four, and she had no doubt that they'd gone through the wall, perhaps even into the kitchen.

Then, it stopped.

"This is Sheriff Dawson," he called out.

Elaina recognized the voice and knew that help had arrived. But at what cost? The sheriff likely hadn't heard the silenced shots from the front of the house, and the man could be ambushed if he got near the shooter.

"The gunman's out back," Luke shouted to the sheriff. "Take cover. I'm going to return fire."

"No!" Elaina whispered. She didn't dare say it any louder because she couldn't alarm Christopher. Nor could she move closer to Luke. It would put the baby at risk.

But Luke took all the risks. He levered himself up, aimed his gun at what was left of the back nursery window and fired. These were not muffled shots but thick, deafening blasts. Elaina hugged Christopher even closer to her and prayed that he wouldn't wake up. While she was at it, she added a prayer that Luke would be okay.

"Halt your fire," the sheriff called out. "I see the shooter. I'm in pursuit."

Luke scrambled into the nursery. Elaina could no longer see him, but she figured he'd moved to the window so he could provide backup for the sheriff if necessary.

She sat there, holding the baby and waiting for all of this to end. She could hear the hum of her clock and Christopher's soft rhythmic breathing. She tried to let that calm her so that she wouldn't be tempted to call out to Luke to make sure he was okay.

"He got away," she heard the sheriff say. He sounded close, perhaps by the nursery window. But just the fact that he was nearby made her breathe easier. The sheriff probably wouldn't be standing in the open if he thought the gunman was still a threat.

"*He?*" Luke questioned. Elaina moved closer to the door so she could better hear the conversation. Thankfully, Luke asked the question that was foremost on her mind. "You're sure it was a man?"

"I'm not sure of that at all. The person was wearing dark clothes. You have a suspect in mind, or any idea why someone would want to do this?"

"I'll go over that with you just as soon as I've checked on Agent Foley."

"I'll do it. You stay put," the sheriff insisted. "Just in case our shooter returns."

So much for breathing easier. And at least from this angle she could see Luke. He wasn't hurt. But he was angry. His jaw muscles were iron stiff, and he seemed primed and ready for a fight. Elaina understood that. Someone had endangered Christopher. Neither Luke nor she would forget that anytime soon.

Luke didn't look back at her. He kept his gun and attention focused on the gaping hole in what was left of the window and the plantation blinds. The gauzy pale blue curtains fluttered around him like ghosts. And beneath his shoes was a thick layer of broken glass. It looked like carnage and chaos.

"This won't go unpunished," she heard Luke say. And she didn't doubt him. What Elaina did doubt was that Luke could catch this shooter and come out of it unharmed.

He would die to protect them.

Two days ago, that would have made her feel safe. Right now, it made her sick to her stomach. She didn't want to deal with the thought of losing him, which was ironic, because Luke Buchanan wasn't hers to lose.

There was a heavy-handed knock at the door. The sound shot through her and made Elaina gasp. Her body prepared for a second round of deadly threats, but she soon realized that wasn't necessary.

"I found Agent Foley," the sheriff shouted. Luke hurried to the front door and opened it. "He's been shot."

Luke cursed. Silently, Elaina did the same thing.

"How bad?" Luke asked.

"He's alive, and I've already called for an ambulance. I'll wait with him."

So, this wasn't over. A federal agent had been shot. If Rusty didn't make it, then they had a killer on their hands. A killer who'd tried his best to murder them tonight.

Why?

Was this really about that damned software? Or Devereux's retaliation? How could anyone risk a baby's life for the sake of money or reprisal?

"Don't come out just yet," Luke instructed. His voice was level, but there was raw emotion in it. He was no doubt thinking of his fellow agent, a man who'd been shot while trying to protect them. "How's Christopher?"

She looked down at him. "Sleeping."

Luke made a sound of approval. "I swear I won't let this happen again."

"You didn't *let* it happen this time," Elaina countered.

She would have said more, probably something sappy and emotional. She no doubt would have gushed her thanks. Gratitude that Luke would have resented because he wouldn't have seen his actions as an option.

But there was another knock at the front door.

"It's Sheriff Dawson," the man said. She heard Luke open the door again. "More bad news."

Chapter Thirteen

Luke waited until he was alone in the bedroom of the safe house before he cursed. He cursed the situation that Elaina and he were in and he cursed the list of things that just kept going wrong.

Most of all he cursed himself.

He should have pushed to get this safe house in San Antonio sooner. That way, Rusty wouldn't have been sitting in front of Elaina's house, he wouldn't have been shot in the chest and he wouldn't now be in the hospital fighting for his life. If they'd been in a safe house, Elaina and Christopher wouldn't have had to go through an attack that could have easily gotten them killed.

Those things were massive mistakes, but there was another by-product of Luke's failure to speed up the safe house process. Because Sheriff Dawson had had to respond to the shooting, that left the jail manned only by a bank security guard who occasionally did duty as an auxiliary deputy. The sheriff estimated there was a half-hour window of time while he and his real deputy were dealing with the aftermath of the shooting that the two prisoners were alone with the security guard.

The two men—the blonde and the guy with the eye patch—had managed to knock out the guard and escape.

Now, they were at large, and that meant in addition to keeping Elaina and Christopher safe, Luke had two more culprits that he had to be on the lookout for.

Yeah. He'd made a mess of things.

Luke was trying to remedy that. He now had Elaina, Christopher and even the sitter, Theresa, settled into a safe house in San Antonio. But that didn't mean they were *safe*. As long as the two escapees and their boss were out there, Elaina and Christopher would be in danger.

He glanced at the computer he'd set up on a fold-up card table. The screen was still blank, which meant the audio feed wasn't coming through yet. But it would. And then Luke would get a chance to do something else that he should have done before he ever visited Elaina…have a chat with George Devereux. And thanks to computer technology that should happen within the next half hour.

There was a soft tap at the door, and he peered over his shoulder as Elaina came in. She'd showered and changed into jeans and a shirt the same honey color as her hair, but she didn't look refreshed. Her eyes were sleep starved, and she looked as stressed out as Luke felt.

Elaina glanced at the computer screen, saw that it was blank and she walked in. But she didn't walk in too far. She kept her distance.

"How's Christopher?" Luke asked.

"He's fine. Theresa's feeding him breakfast. It was a really a good idea to bring her here with us. It's nice to have the extra pair of hands."

Well, that was one reason Luke included Theresa in their rushed evacuation of Crystal Creek. The other reason was that he was concerned that the escapees would go to the sitter's house and try to get her to tell them where Elaina was. Theresa was likely in as much danger as the rest of them. Maybe more since she wouldn't be able to defend herself.

"The hospital just called Agent Culpepper," Elaina told him.

That got Luke's attention. Agent Culpepper was the guard assigned to the safe house. A man that Luke trusted. Thankfully, Culpepper was in the living room and would stay there throughout this ordeal. "Is Rusty—"

"He made it through surgery and is in stable condition," Elaina interrupted. "The doctors think he'll make a full recovery."

Luke released the breath he didn't even know he'd been holding. That was one thing knocked off his mental list of concerns. Still, Rusty shouldn't have been put through this.

"What about the escapees?" Luke wanted to know. "Has anyone called Agent Culpepper about them?"

She shook her head and walked to the window where he was standing. Like him, she peered out at the morning sun and the empty sidewalk of the sleepy middle-class neighborhood. "But Culpepper did say that the Justice Department was involved in the search. Maybe that'll speed things up and get them back behind bars where they belong."

"That can't happen soon enough. These are the men who tried to kill you last year."

"But it wasn't them last night," she commented. She turned, faced him and raked her fingers through the side of her hair. "I've been trying to piece it together, and I think we're back to square one."

Luke nodded. Frowned. Cursed. Because he'd come to the same god-awful conclusion. "Gary, Brenda, Carrie or George Devereux. Any one of them could be behind what happened. Maybe none of them was the actual shooter, but they could have hired someone to do it."

"True. But were they merely trying to create a diversion so the prisoners could escape?" Elaina asked.

Luke wished that were the only reason, but he suspected something much more sinister. "With you and me out of the way, it would be much easier to search your house."

"Of course." She waited a moment, obviously trying to grasp and get past that. "What about the background checks you did on the suspects? Any news?"

He shook his head. "I talked to the investigator early this morning before you got up." At least he thought it was before that. Elaina and Christopher had stayed in one room. Theresa, in another. Luke had ended up in the third bedroom, where he'd spent the night mentally kicking himself.

"And?" she prompted.

"Gary has those mysterious funds in his account, but he claims it was repayment of an old loan from a college buddy. Nothing financial has popped up in Brenda's files yet, but the investigator can't rule her out, especially since Brenda moved to Crystal Creek just a few months ago."

"They didn't find anything on Carrie, either." It wasn't exactly a question.

Unfortunately, Luke had an answer that Elaina wouldn't be pleased to hear. He certainly hadn't been thrilled about it. "Were you aware that Carrie recently started using one of those prepaid cell phones that aren't traceable?"

Elaina shrugged. "That's not a crime. She's always on a tight budget. She probably ran up too big of a bill on her last phone and had to switch to something cheaper."

"Maybe. But the Justice Department isn't quite as trusting as you are. Carrie left the cell phone behind in the Crystal Creek diner yesterday, Rusty spotted it, and he sent it to the crime lab to see if we can retrieve any of the numbers she called."

"I'm sure you won't find anything incriminating," she insisted.

Luke didn't give up. He continued with the next bit of info he'd learned about her assistant. "Two weeks ago, Carrie applied to Rice University in Houston for their summer term. Did you know about that?"

She blinked, and it took a moment for her to answer. "No. Well, I knew she wanted to take art classes, but she said that she couldn't afford them."

"Well, she can apparently afford it now, which means that Carrie might be on the verge of a big payoff for locating that miniature memory chip that Kevin used to store his modifications."

Elaina folded her arms over her chest and stepped back. "I just can't believe she'd do something like this."

Luke understood that skepticism, but he wasn't about to cut Elaina's shop assistant any slack. Carrie was a suspect, and he would treat her as such.

Behind them, Luke heard a voice, and he turned to see the image of an agent on the screen. "The video interview has been set up," the agent informed Luke. "Are you ready to speak with inmate George Devereux?"

"Give me a second." Luke caught on to Elaina's arm and moved her to the corner of the room so that she'd be out of camera range. "I need you to stay quiet." He didn't want Devereux to know that Elaina was with him. It was best to give his old nemesis as little information as possible.

Luke sat down at the computer, glanced over the

notes he'd made earlier and he gave the nod to the agent. There was a flicker on the screen, mere seconds passed, and he saw the face of a man that Luke had hoped he'd never see again. It wasn't easy, but Luke put a chokehold on his anger. However, if he learned that Devereux had had some part in the shooting, that chokehold would snap.

Devereux didn't look like a beaten man. In fact, he looked pampered. He had a good haircut. No signs of aging, even though the man was in his early sixties. Luke hoped that didn't mean that Devereux had used part of his multimillion dollar estate to bribe a guard or two.

"Agent Buchanan," Devereux greeted. "I'm missing my midmorning workout."

Luke considered some smart-mouth response, but he held back. "I've been going over a list of your visitors and call sheets. Your daughter, Genevieve, has phoned the prison six times in the past month. Your conversations were unsupervised."

Devereux shrugged. "Because she's acting as my legal counsel."

Yes, that's what the guard's note had said. "But she's not a lawyer."

"I can designate anyone to legally represent me." His cobalt-blue eyes seemed to pierce right through the screen. "Agent Buchanan, if you have plans to go after my daughter—"

"Has she done anything that warrants an arrest?" Luke quipped.

"No. And I won't have you try to use her to get back at me. What happened between us is finished."

Luke was more than a little surprised with that comment. He'd expected Devereux to be defensive. Irate, even. But the man seemed to be protecting his daughter.

Now that he had Christopher, Luke totally understood that reaction. He glanced at Elaina who was nibbling on her bottom lip. Yep. She understood it, too. It gave people a bond that might not always be a good bond to have, but that was a thought for another time, another place.

"I just wanted to make sure you weren't using your daughter for more than legal council," Luke continued.

Devereux's reaction was mild, a slight tilt of the head. "Such as?"

"Perhaps Genevieve is doing your dirty work. There was a shooting last night. What do you know about that?"

Devereux sat there amid the dust-gray walls and stared at him. "I know nothing about it. Neither does Genevieve. My daughter is trying to start a family, Agent Buchanan. The only thing she has on her mind is motherhood. I want it to stay that way. Under no circumstance will you bring any of this to her, understand?"

"Fine. Then, give me the answers I'm looking for, and I won't have to go to her."

"What answers?" Devereux snapped.

"Have you been in the market for some software modifications?"

Devereux paused as if absorbing that, smiled and shook his head. "No. I'm not a computer person. I hire people to do that sort of thing for me."

That wasn't the answer Luke was looking for. "Are you saying one of your employees was in the market?"

"I'm not saying that all, but I wouldn't have any use for software modifications unless those modifications can reverse the prison sentence that put me in this place. That's my concern right now. That and my daughter. I've put my business ventures on hold."

Either Devereux was a convincing liar, or he was telling the truth. It might be a while before Luke figured out which, but for the time being, he was going to treat the man as he was treating Carrie and the others.

Like a suspect who wanted Elaina and him dead.

"How about your investment in the Brighton Birthing Center?" Luke questioned.

Devereux relaxed his shoulders. "Oh, that. The police were already here first thing this morning. I'll tell you what I told them. I make lots of investments, and I chose that one when my daughter informed me that she was interested in starting a family. I knew the former director at Brighton, I believed her to be an honest woman, and I learned the hard way that she wasn't. She was behind many of those illegal adoptions and even once tried to kill a police officer."

That meshed with the phone briefing Luke had gotten with San Antonio PD. There didn't appear to be anything sinister about Devereux's investment, but Luke would keep digging. If there was anything to find, he'd find it.

"Talk to me about my late wife," Luke insisted. He debated how to go with this and decided to take the direct approach. "Did you have anything to do with her death?"

"No. But I doubt you'll believe me." Devereux made a dismissal wave of his hand. "I'm a family man, Agent Buchanan. My problem is with you, not any member of your family."

"But you could have tried to get to me by going through my family," Luke quickly pointed out.

The man sighed dramatically. "That would create bad karma. And what purpose would it serve? It would only cause you to hound and harass me, and since I will almost certainly have my sentence reversed on appeal, why would I do anything to keep you on my tail?"

Luke could think of reasons. "For money, power or both."

"I already have those things in spades." But there was no smugness in his tone. Devereux had said merely as fact. "Has someone been trying to connect me to this software and your dead wife?"

"Me. I've been trying to do just that. She gave birth to a child at Brighton."

"I've never stepped foot in the place," Devereux insisted. "There is no connection between your wife and me."

"I hope, for your sake, there isn't."

"Investigate to your heart's desire, but you won't find my metaphorical fingerprints anywhere near your late wife."

Luke stared at the man, wondering if he'd get a different answer if he kept pushing, but Luke instinctively knew that he wouldn't. He didn't bother to say goodbye. Luke used the computer mouse to end the video call, and he clicked back to the agent who'd set up the connection.

The face of the agent reappeared on the screen. "Monitor all his visits," Luke insisted. "Report anything suspicious directly to me." Luke turned off the computer and looked at Elaina.

"Is Devereux a good liar?" she asked.

He stood, shook his head. "He's capable of lying, but I wouldn't say he's good at it."

Elaina huffed and clenched her hands into fists. "I just want answers. I want to know why someone is trying to kill us."

"We'll figure that out. In the meantime, Christopher is safe."

"But for how long?" But she didn't just say it; her voice trembled.

Luke walked closer.

"If it were just me at risk, it wouldn't hurt like this," she whispered. "But Christopher. God, Christopher could be in danger."

Oh, yeah. He understood that all too well. "I'm not going to let anything happen to him."

She looked up at him, and he could feel the attraction rear its head. The last time, though, that he'd acted on that attraction had been minutes before the shooting. If he hadn't been making out with Elaina in the hall, he might have spotted the gunman before he took aim.

And that was the reason Luke didn't go any closer.

"What's wrong?" she asked. But she lifted her hand, palm out in a *stop* gesture. "This is the conversation we were about to have after we nearly had sex. You backed away from me then, too. Not physically, but I could feel it." She paused. "Luke, that had nothing to do with me trying to keep custody of Christopher."

"I know it didn't." And it was time for him to apologize. His lust had nearly gotten her killed.

But the apology was put on hold when his phone rang. Since it could be an update on Rusty or the escaped prisoners, Luke quickly answered it.

"It's Sheriff Dawson. I have a problem. My wife was in a car accident. Nothing serious, but the doctor here wants to transfer her to the hospital in Luling for a CAT scan. I have to leave to be with her."

"How can I help?"

"Well, I have no one to cover my office, and I have a prisoner. A man I had to arrest this morning for taking a baseball bat to his brother. I can't leave him here alone, and I don't trust the security guard who let the other two escape."

Neither did Luke. "What about your deputy?"

"He's at Elaina's house still standing guard so no

one will get inside, but I've got to pull him from that duty and have him come here to the station. I've called the sheriff in a neighboring county, and he's planning to send some help, but it'd go easier for me if you could go to Elaina's house and stand guard until the federal agents show up to search the place."

The mental debate started, but it wasn't much of a debate. Those federal agents were likely tied up with apprehending the escaped prisoners. Plus, Elaina's house needed to be searched, and it needed to be guarded. He couldn't risk any of their suspects getting in to search for Kevin's software modifications—especially since they'd left critical items in the car in the garage when they'd made a mad dash to get out of there and come to safe house. Luke needed to find the modifications to discover the identity of T. They might be the key to making sure Elaina and Christopher were truly safe.

Luke checked his watch. "I'll be there in about two hours," he assured the sheriff.

Sheriff Dawson thanked him and hung up.

"Where are you going?" Elaina asked.

"To your house. The deputy guarding it is being pulled. I'll wait for backup to arrive, and while I'm doing that, I'll search the place."

"I could help you."

He was already shaking his head before she finished. "Too dangerous."

"It's broad daylight, and the search will go faster if there are two of us. Besides, I know what I brought to the house from San Antonio. You don't. For you, it'd be like a needle in a haystack."

"Those two men are on the loose," Luke quickly reminded her.

"Those two men have been on the loose for over a year," Elaina reminded him. "Christopher could stay here with Theresa, where they'll be safe. I could watch your back. You could watch mine."

She was right about one thing—the search would go a hell of a lot faster if she was there with him.

"It makes sense," she argued. "If we don't find anything in a couple of hours, then you can bring me back. Five hours," she said, obviously bargaining now.

Luke debated with himself some more. He weighted the consequences. And he finally nodded. "Five hours."

"I'll get my purse and tell Theresa."

Luke reached for his shoulder holster and gun. He prayed he wouldn't need it, and while he was praying, he added one more thing.

He hoped he wasn't leading Elaina right back into the path of a killer.

Chapter Fourteen

Elaina finished her call to Theresa and told Luke what she'd learned. "Christopher just finished eating his snack, and Theresa is about to put him down for his nap."

"How long will he sleep?" Luke asked.

"At least an hour, maybe longer. Don't worry. Christopher is used to being with Theresa all day. He won't be upset that I'm not there."

"Good. That's one less thing to worry about."

Yes, one less thing.

She checked her watch. What would have normally been a forty-five-minute drive to her house turned into nearly double that amount of time.

Before they'd even gotten in the car, Luke had told her that he would have to take a circuitous route to make sure they weren't being followed, and he was true to his word. One hour and fifty minutes after they'd kissed Christopher goodbye and drove away from the safe house, they finally pulled into her driveway.

"What now?" Luke mumbled when he saw the activity in front of them.

Elaina had expected to see yellow crime scene tape stretched around her property. And it was there, being assaulted by the winter wind. She'd also expected to see boarded up windows, and someone had indeed taken care of that chore. But her expectations hadn't stopped there. She'd expected to see a deputy or some other law enforcement official.

That, she didn't see.

But Gary was on her front porch, his hand poised in the air as if he were about to knock on the door.

Luke obviously didn't care for Gary's presence because he slammed on the brakes and came to a loud, screeching halt mere inches from the porch steps. That got Gary's attention. The man whirled around to face them, and he certainly looked guilty of something.

"Wait in the car," Luke told her. In the same motion, he drew his gun and got out. "This is crime scene, and you're trespassing."

Elaina lowered the window so she could hear everything they were saying.

"I, uh, know, but I saw the deputy leave, and I wanted to make sure Elaina wasn't here alone," Gary insisted.

"She's not."

"Oh. Okay." He peered into the car and waved at her. That was friendly enough, but the glare he turned on Luke wasn't so friendly. "You can put that gun away."

Luke didn't. "How long has the deputy been gone?"

"Fifteen, maybe twenty minutes. I was watching out the window, and when I saw him drive away, I got dressed and came over."

"To make sure Elaina wasn't here alone," Luke repeated, and he sounded totally skeptical.

"The crime scene guys have been here. They've already processed the house and the grounds," Gary continued.

"*Processed?*" More skepticism and a lot of suspicion from Luke.

"I watch a lot of cop shows," Gary explained. "That's the term they use."

"It's the right term," Luke verified. "But if you watch cop shows, then you know you should never step foot in a crime scene. Go home, Gary, and stay away until you hear otherwise from me."

Gary took a step toward Luke, and there was nothing submissive about it. Elaina noted the combative stance that was no doubt a result of his military training.

"I'm not sure why Elaina ever married you," Gary said, moving even closer to Luke.

"That's not your concern. Go. Home," Luke repeated.

The two men stood there, as if sizing each other up, but with Luke armed, Gary must have decided this wasn't a fight he could win. He lifted his hands in a suit-yourself gesture, cursed and stormed off the porch. Luke didn't take his eyes off him until Gary was back in his own house.

"You can get out now," Luke let Elaina know.

He carried that edgy, dangerous tone through to what he said to her. But once their eyes met, something inside him settled. Well, a little anyway. Luke lowered his gun a fraction, but he eased her behind him while they approached the front door.

"That deputy shouldn't have left until I got here," Luke mumbled. "Another minute or two and Gary would have probably been inside snooping around."

Luke tested the doorknob and cursed. "It's unlocked."

Elaina groaned. It was bad enough that the deputy had left early, but it was careless to leave the place unlocked. Of course, with all activity from the crime scene guys, it wouldn't have been difficult for someone to sneak in.

And then she heard the sound of someone talking.

Luke obviously did, as well. He pushed her to the side and threw open the door. Despite Luke's attempt to keep her out of the line of fire, Elaina could see inside her house.

Carrie was in her living room.

"What are you doing here?" Luke demanded.

Carrie turned toward them and froze. That's when Elaina saw that her assistant had the phone in her hand. Not her own personal phone but Elaina's house phone.

"Elaina," Carrie said, the breath all in her voice. She put down the phone and stared at Luke's gun. "I used the emergency key you gave me to let myself in."

Luke gave her a questioning glance, and Elaina nodded to verify that she had indeed given Carrie a key.

"I was trying to call you." Carrie hitched her shoulder toward the phone. "I can't find my cell phone."

And Elaina knew why. When Luke had first told her that the Justice Department had an interest in Carrie's phone, Elaina had totally dismissed it. But since the shooting, she wasn't feeling nearly as trusting, and she wasn't dismissing it now.

Carrie rushed to her and gave her a hard hug. "God, I heard about the shooting, but I had no idea it was this bad. There's glass everywhere in the kitchen and nursery. Are Christopher and you all right?"

"We're fine." Elaina pulled away so she could face Carrie. "But you shouldn't be here."

Carrie nodded. "I know, but I was so scared when I heard the news. I couldn't stay away." She looked around the room. "Maybe I can help you clean up the place."

"It can't be cleaned yet," Luke insisted. He reholstered his gun, but he kept his hand on it. "You really should go."

Carrie nodded, but she didn't look in total agreement. "Okay, but call me if you need anything."

"I will." But Elaina knew she wouldn't. Not unless her assistant was cleared as a suspect.

The moment that Carrie was out the door, Luke locked it and engaged the security system. He didn't stop there. He stormed through the house, checking each room. It wasn't a speedy process because he looked in every closet and beneath the beds. Apparently satisfied that no one else had let themselves in, he went to her phone. The one that Carrie had been using when they walked in.

Elaina watched as he pressed redial, and he held the phone between so both of them could hear. There were four rings before the answering machine kicked in. "Hi, you've reached Brenda. I'm not here right now, but leave a message at the beep."

Luke dropped the phone back into the cradle.

"Brenda," Elaina and he repeated in unison.

It was Elaina who continued. "Maybe Carrie thought Brenda would know how to get in touch with me."

"Or maybe she was giving Brenda an update of what she did or didn't find in the house. Maybe the women are working together for this T person."

Elaina's imagination began to run wild. She'd worked side by side with Carrie for a year, but did that mean anything? Carrie was being secretive about her application to Rice. Why wouldn't Carrie tell her something like that, especially since the woman discussed everything else with Elaina?

"But I don't know what Carrie would have found that I couldn't," Elaina commented.

"We left the box of files in the car in the garage," Luke reminded her. "She might have been trying to get another peek at them. Don't worry. That box won't be staying here. I'm taking it back with us to the safe house. We'll go over the files tonight."

"While we're here, I'll get some clothes and things. We didn't have much with us when we left."

Dreading what she knew she would see, Elaina went into the nursery. Carrie had been right. There was glass all over the floor and markings on the wall to indicate where bullets had been removed. It was sickening. Her baby's room was now a crime scene.

"I won't be able to live here again," Elaina said softly. But she obviously didn't say it nearly soft enough.

"I understand," Luke responded.

She looked over her shoulder at him. He was close. Very close. And he was watching her.

"I'll be okay," she insisted.

"Are you trying to convince me, or yourself?"

She frowned at his astute observation. Even though Luke hadn't known her long, he obviously *knew* her. Maybe all the danger and forced camaraderie could do that. Maybe that's why she felt so connected to him.

Luke reached out and pulled her into his arms. She felt stronger and weaker all at the same time. She also felt as if she owed him a gigantic thank-you.

"Despite the dramatic and crazy intrusion you made into my fake life, I'm glad you're here and on my side," Elaina confessed.

She would deal with the consequences of his presence after all of this was over. And she had no doubt that there would be consequences.

Since his arms were giving her a little too much comfort, and since the closeness was a reminder of how hotly attracted she was to him, Elaina eased back slightly. "I'll start going through the things in my bedroom."

He nodded and let her slip out of his embrace. Just like that, she felt the loss, and she cursed herself for it. She wasn't just getting close to Luke; she was falling hard for him.

And that couldn't happen.

Hadn't her disastrous relationship with Kevin taught her anything? She had lousy taste in men, and Luke might be good father material, but he'd made it clear that he wasn't looking for a personal involvement with her.

Well, at least he'd made it clear in the beginning. But maybe like her, he'd had a change of heart.

It was stupid, but that caused her to smile, and she carried that smile into her bedroom to begin the search. The smile soon faded. The room looked almost exactly the way they'd left it. The mattress was on the floor where Luke had left it. Pictures had been knocked off the dresser.

Elaina walked past all of that and went into her closet. She did a quick inventory to figure out if she'd brought any of the items with her when she fled her old life. She'd already given Luke the files and a few other things, but she went through each item of clothing and each pair of shoes. It didn't take her long to decide that all of her things were less than a year old. Because she'd been running for her life at the time, she hadn't brought much with her.

Giving up on the closet, she went into the bathroom to check her cosmetics. Again, this room was as they'd left it, with a bath towel draped across the edge of the sink. It was next to Luke's leather toiletry bag. Elaina started to stoop to look in the cabinet beneath the sink, but something in the unzipped toiletry bag caught her eye.

A small square-shaped gold-foil packet.

Elaina actually picked it up to verify what it was. Though it wasn't necessary. She knew it was a condom.

She felt as if someone had slapped her.

Her thought raced back to the night before, to the hot and heavy kissing session in the hall. Luke and she had nearly had sex. In fact, the only thing that had stopped him was there was no condom.

Or so he'd said.

But this proved otherwise.

Mercy, had he lied to her? Elaina didn't want to believe that. In fact, she refused to believe it. Luke had been just as aroused and ready as she'd been. If he'd known about the condom, he would have used it.

Wouldn't he?

Elaina didn't have time to ponder that particular question because there was a frantic knock at the door. She rushed out of the bathroom to find Luke already on his way to the front of the house. He had his gun drawn.

He motioned for Elaina to duck back in the bedroom, and she did. But she stayed near the door so she could see what was happening.

"Who's there?" Luke called out.

"Me, Brenda."

Elaina didn't know whether to groan or curse. Obviously, her friends, neighbors and possible enemies weren't concerned about traipsing onto a crime scene.

"Guys?" Brenda's pounding became louder and more insistent. "You really need to let me in *now*."

"Why?" Luke answered.

"Because there are two people sitting in a car just a half block up. I got a glimpse inside as I jogged past them, and both are armed. Elaina, I think your shooter is back."

Chapter Fifteen

Luke didn't open the door. Instead, he went to the window and looked out. There was indeed a dark green two-door car parked just up the block.

Because he didn't want to risk Brenda being shot, nor did he want to put Elaina at risk, he didn't lower his gun, but he went to the front door, disengaged the security system and opened it. Brenda was there, looking a little harried and sweaty despite the near freezing temperatures.

Brenda had her hand in the pocket of her jogging jacket, and Luke made an immediate assessment that there was something wrong with her body language and stance. He caught on to her arm, hauled her inside and reached into her pocket. He retrieved a small handgun.

"What are you doing with this?" he demanded.

"Isn't it obvious?" She pointed in the direction of the car. "There's a shooter on the loose, and I wasn't going to take any chances."

Neither was Luke. He kept her gun and didn't plan to return it until Brenda was on her way out. Even then, she might not get it back.

"Call the sheriff's office," Luke instructed Elaina. "Let them know we might have a problem."

However, before Elaina could pick up the phone, Luke's own cell phone rang. He handed Brenda's gun to Elaina and answered it. He was careful though not to use his name because as far as he knew, Brenda still thought he was Daniel Allen. Luke wanted to keep it that way for a while so it would save him from being asked too many questions.

"Agent Buchanan," the caller said. "This is Collena Drake. I saw your visitor and thought I should wait for her to leave before I come up to the house."

"You're in the two-door dark green car?" Luke asked.

"Yes. I came with a Justice Department agent. He's going to guard the place while Elaina and you are here."

Luke was relieved to hear those words. "I wouldn't say no to that." He paused. "Why'd you come to Crystal Creek?"

"We have something important to discuss."

No relieved feeling this time. He didn't like the sound of that. "I was just showing our guest out anyway. Give me a couple of minutes."

Brenda flinched. "What do you mean you're showing me out? I can't go out there. The gunman—"

"That's a federal agent and a former cop in the car. You'll be safe." He glanced at Elaina to let her know that the safety extended to her. "But, Brenda, I would like to know why you're here."

She squared her shoulders. "For Elaina, of course. I was worried about her."

"There's a lot of that going around," Luke mumbled.

Here, he'd thought Elaina and he were going to get some quality search time, and instead they'd been bombarded with people. The only one he wanted to see was Collena Drake. She wouldn't have come unless she had important information.

"I'll go," Brenda offered. "But just tell me where you're staying so I'll know how to get in touch with you."

"We'll be at my sister's in Arkansas," Luke readily answered.

It was obviously a lie, since he didn't even have a sister, but a lie was as good as Brenda was going to get.

"Okay." Brenda nodded. "So, you're not planning on staying here?"

"No," Elaina answered. "But there'll be someone guarding the place until the investigation is finished."

Another nod, this one was a little choppy. Brenda went to Elaina her and hugged her. She did the same to Luke, surprising him. And alarming him. He didn't like a suspect being so close to his gun.

And speaking of guns, he had to take care of the matter of what to do with Brenda's. Legally, he had no right to confiscate it. So, he walked Brenda to the door and handed her the weapon once they were outside on the porch.

"Who's out there in the car?" Elaina asked the moment Luke closed the door behind Brenda.

"An agent and Collena Drake."

The color drained from her face. "She's not here to take Christopher?"

"Nothing like that." But he couldn't say what this conversation would entail.

He walked to the front window and looked out. So did Elaina. She stood right beside him. "Collena will come in soon," Luke explained. "She just wants to make sure Brenda is gone first."

Elaina didn't say a word.

"Is anything wrong?" he asked. When the silence continued, he added another question. "Did you find anything in your bedroom?"

"Sort of. But it doesn't apply to the investigation. It's personal." She paused. "We can discuss it after you talk to Ms. Drake."

"That sounds ominous." Another glance out the window, and he confirmed that Collena still hadn't gotten out of the car. "It must really be bad."

She opened her mouth, closed it and she stayed that way several moments before she finally spoke. "When I was in the bathroom, I saw a condom in your toiletry bag."

It took him a moment to put two and two together.

Hell.

Luke tried to explain but soon realized he didn't have a clue what to say. However, Elaina didn't have any problem in that area.

"You know, if you didn't want to have sex with me, that's all you had to say." She folded her arms over her chest and glared at him. "What I got from you was a pity orgasm, and I don't appreciate that."

"There was no pity. Not on my part anyway."

Oh, man. That was not the right thing to say. Her eyes narrowed, and her teeth came together. "It wasn't pity on my part, either. I wasn't playing a game while we were in the hall. Every emotion was real."

"I know."

"Do you?" she snapped. "Because I think you still believe that I'm trying to manipulate you into sharing custody of Christopher with me."

Now that riled him. "I don't think you'd use sex to do that, and trust me, I wouldn't have kissed you or touched you if I'd thought that was on your mind. I might be attracted to you, but I don't do all my thinking below the belt."

"Then why lie about the condom?" she asked.

Well, he couldn't just fire off an answer to that one. And it didn't matter how he said this, it wasn't going to sound good. Not to Elaina.

Probably not to himself, either.

"I didn't want to lose focus on the investigation," he told her. But that was only half the story, and judging from Elaina's expression, she knew that. She deserved better. She deserved to hear the truth. "I was a terrible husband to Taylor. I was never there when she needed me."

"And you thought…what—that I was looking for

a husband? I'm a grown woman, and not once did I think you'd owe a marriage proposal if we had sex."

Luke met her gaze. "But I thought maybe you'd think it was more than sex."

She threw her hands up in the air. "Mercy! You don't have much faith and trust in me. Don't answer that. I know. I know. You really don't know me well enough to have faith." Elaina shook her head. "Luke, it's all right if you don't want a sexual relationship or for that matter, any other kind of relationship with me. Heck, I'm not sure I want one with you. But please don't lie to me again. I've had enough of Kevin's lies to last me a lifetime."

"See? And that's the point. We both have so much baggage. That's why I didn't go get that condom."

She stayed quiet a moment. "I guess that's the bottom line. Neither of us might be able to get past our pasts. At least I know where I stand now."

No, she didn't. Heck, Luke didn't know where he stood. Or what he felt. He just knew that this wasn't the time or the place. They had to concentrate on finding the people who wanted them dead. That was it.

That was the real bottom line.

Luke saw some movement out of the corner of his eye, and he spotted Collena Drake making her way across the yard toward the house. The conversation would have to wait.

He glanced at Elaina to tell her that, but her attention was already on the tall, rail-thin blonde approaching the porch steps. Collena was dressed in black pants and a turtleneck. Her calf-length leather coat was black, too. Ditto for the dark sunglasses. She looked as if she could have been on her way to a funeral, but each time Luke had seen her, she'd worn a similar outfit.

"So this is the person…." But Elaina didn't finish that. Instead, she looked away.

Luke mentally finished the sentence for her. Elaina no doubt felt that Collena had ruined her life. Because Collena had helped him find his son, Luke had an entirely different opinion of the woman.

He opened the door to her, and they exchanged brief smiles as she entered. However, there was no joy in Collena Drake's smile. She introduced herself to Elaina and pulled off those sunglasses. There was no joy there, either. Luke was betting that a lot of heart-breaking sadness had put that emotion in her brown eyes.

"I won't stay long," Collena started. She shook her head, declining to sit on the sofa when Elaina motioned in that direction. "I'll tell you both what I've learned because it applies to this investigation." But her eyes landed on Luke when she continued. "You know that the police exhumed your late wife's body."

Luke nodded. "They're conducting another autopsy."

She brought out an envelope from her pocket. "The coroner is finished. He did me a favor and put a rush on it."

Luke took it and stared at it.

"I can give you the gist of it," Collena said when he didn't open it. "Taylor died from complications from a C-section. Basically, she got an infection, and her body didn't respond to antibiotics. The infection caused organ damage and then kidney failure."

Oh, man. That was hard to hear, but it also gave Luke some consolation. At least it didn't appear to be murder.

"So that lets George Devereux off the hook," Elaina concluded.

Collena nodded. "The coroner checked for negligence on the part of the hospital staff. In other words, they might have not taken full measures to stop the infection. His results are inconclusive. We might never know the answer."

Yeah. And somehow Luke would have to learn to live with that. At the moment, however, he wasn't even sure that was possible.

Since he had no choice, Luke sank down on the arm of the sofa. Elaina immediately went to him. She touched his arm and rubbed gently.

"Devereux might be off the hook," Elaina said. "But that doesn't explain who tried to kill us last night."

Collena nodded. "The SAPD have a theory for that, too. The day that Luke came to Crystal Creek, two men matching the description of the guy with the eye patch and his blond partner were seen near the Cryogen Lab in San Antonio."

Oh, this was not sounding good. "That's where I took Christopher's pacifier for the DNA test."

"Yes. The police reviewed surveillance tapes, and they spotted the men in the parking lot just minutes before you picked up the test results. It looks as if they were waiting for you and perhaps even followed you."

Luke shook his head. He was about to say that he would have noticed the men, especially if they'd followed him, but the truth was, he wasn't sure of that. Seeing those DNA results had felt like sucker punch. It'd confirmed his worst fears and his greatest wish.

"How would these men have known to follow Luke?" Elaina asked.

"Maybe through the information I was posting about the investigation on my Web site," Collena explained. "I have information there for parents who are still searching for their lost children. The two men could have realized that Luke was looking for you and his son, and they perhaps wanted to use Luke to get to you."

He pushed his thumb against his chest. "I'm responsible for those men finding Elaina and Christopher." He moved away when Elaina tried to continue to rub his arm. It was a loving gesture meant to soothe him, but he wasn't in the mood to be soothed. He damn sure didn't deserve any loving gestures from the very woman he'd nearly gotten killed.

"I'm sorry," Collena said. "I wish there'd been an easier way to tell you this."

She added a soft goodbye and quietly left.

Since Luke wasn't sure he could move yet, he was thankful when Elaina went to the door to lock it and re-arm the security system. With his state of mind, he needed all the help he could get.

"Well, at least we know Devereux's not the one who's after us," Elaina commented. She sounded hesitant as if she didn't know what else to say.

Luke was right there, on the same page with her.

She walked closer, also hesitantly, and stopped just a few inches away. She didn't reach out, didn't touch, she just stood there until he looked at her.

"Say it," Luke demanded. "Or slap me. Do something, anything, because I damn well deserve that and worse. I did this." He pointed toward the boarded windows in the kitchen. "I nearly got you killed."

"No. A gunman nearly got us killed."

Sympathy. Luke wasn't in the mood for it. "I brought them to your doorstep."

Elaina shrugged. "They would have found me eventually."

"You don't know that," he fired back.

"Oh, but I do. Remember, I lived with a criminal so I know how they think. Those software modifications are obviously worth a lot, and this T and his henchmen weren't going to give up their search."

Now, she touched him, putting her hand on his shoulder. "Look, I know you're beating yourself up, and I doubt I can say or do anything to convince you otherwise, so just listen. Those men would have found me. Now, what if that had happened after you'd taken Christopher and were no longer around? I seriously doubt the shooter would have been content to fire through the windows. No. The shooter would have waited for a clean shot and would have killed me so he or she could walk inside and search the place."

He wanted to refute that. Man, did he. He wanted to slap this blame right back in his own face. But he couldn't. Not about that particular point anyway. Because Elaina was right. These guys had taken massive risks with the shooting, and people like that usually did whatever it took to get the job done.

That put a fistlike grip around his heart. He could almost see it. Elaina alone under attack.

She put her other hand on his arm and curved her fingers around his bicep. "You know what I'm saying is true."

He didn't nod, didn't agree and he couldn't get those images of her out of his head.

"There are a lot worse things in life than having you here with me," Elaina said, her voice whispery and filled with breath.

He felt the same about her.

But Luke didn't dare say that to her. The air was already charged with the emotion of what they'd learned and with the argument they'd had moments before Collena's arrival. Added to that emotion was Elaina's attempt to make him feel better. She was being caring and sympathetic. Worse, Luke felt in need of some of that caring, even if he didn't deserve it. And there was no doubt about it—he didn't deserve anything but Elaina's wrath and anger.

She apparently didn't feel the same way.

Elaina leaned in and touched her lips to his. It barely qualified as a kiss, but it still packed a punch. Luke felt that punch in every inch of his body, and he knew it was time to move away and resume the search.

Then, she kissed him again.

It was more than a touch this time. Actually, it was more than a kiss. He could feel her hand trembling on his arm. Her mouth was trembling, too. He pulled back to see the tears in her eyes. Those tears cut him to the bone.

"I'm sorry," he told her. "I'm so sorry."

"So am I."

He shook his head, not understanding what she meant. "You have nothing to be sorry for."

"You've forgotten that I illegally have your son. True, it was Kevin who started the process, but once I saw Christopher, I didn't ask questions that I should have asked."

Luke was not going to let her go there. He stood and pulled her into his arms. "This is my blame-fest, and you've done nothing wrong. I know that now."

She looked up at him and blinked back the tears. One escaped though and slid down her cheek.

Luke couldn't bear to see it there, and he kissed it away.

And then for no reason that he could ever justify as logical, he kissed *her*.

The change in both of them was instant. Even if he hadn't been touching her, he would have noticed it. Whatever it was, it was intoxicating. His body shifted into a totally different gear, and everything inside him insisted that he continue to kiss Elaina.

So Luke went with that. He kissed her. It was slow and hungry. He took things from her that he hadn't even known he needed.

She pulled back slightly, looked at him and blinked. What she didn't do was stop or try to move away. She just seemed to be assessing the situation. Something was going to happen between them. Something that neither of them believed should happen. But it was as if they no longer had a say in it.

They stood there for heaven knows how long. Minutes, maybe longer. The rhythm of her heart seemed to fall into cadence with the pulse that throbbed in his wrist.

And the world seemed to just melt away.

"If we just do this fast," she whispered. "We won't have to think about it."

"True."

And it was tempting. Something wild and mindless. Sex against the wall. A frantic coupling that would leave them both exhausted and perhaps even sated.

But he knew it could be more than that. Much more. And maybe that was what they needed. A slow burn that would still leave them exhausted and satisfied, but would also keep her in his arms longer. For some reason that Luke didn't want to explore, that suddenly seemed like the most important thing that could happen between them.

"It won't be fast," he promised her. He drew her to him and kissed her forehead. Her cheek. Her jaw.

"Is that wise?" she asked.

"No."

But then, they were past the point of no return. So, Luke did the only thing he could do. He slid his arm around her waist, eased her closer and kissed her as if this would be the first and the last kiss they'd ever have.

WHAT WAS HAPPENING to her?

Elaina could barely think, but she could feel. Mercy, could she ever feel. It was so odd. The passion and need were there. She had no doubts about that. With just that kiss, Luke took her body from being interested to being desperate for him.

But there was something else.

Something simmering just beneath the surface that she couldn't identify. Maybe this was about the need to comfort each other, the need to try to heal the wound that had been ripped open all over again. It would have been so much easier if it'd been just sex. But Elaina needed to melt into his arms. She needed to feel that all would be right with them.

She needed Luke.

And he apparently needed her.

As if he had all the time in the world, he circled his arm around her waist. He touched his mouth to hers. Slow and lingering. Tender.

Elaina hadn't expected the tenderness.

She obviously hadn't expected a lot of things, including the slow, leisurely way that he lifted her shirt and eased it over her head. He dropped it on the sofa and began to lead her in the direction of her bedroom.

She went willingly.

Elaina tried to return the pleasure that he was giving her with his mouth, but Luke skimmed a finger down her bare skin, tracing her spine all the way down. That robbed her of her breath, and the heat rolled through her.

Did he know what this was doing to her?

Absolutely.

It was a slow, easy slide into the depths of passion.

He took that clever mouth to her neck. More kisses. He used his tongue and gently nipped her. Soon, Elaina was on fire. She wanted to touch him. She wanted to make love to him as he was doing to her.

She put her hands on his chest and slid her fingers over the taut muscles. He was solid. All man. Not that she needed to touch him to know that.

Because her body was already aching for him, she rubbed against him. He had an erection, and she rubbed against it, too, and had the thrill of hearing him suck in his breath.

He stopped them just short of the bed. He leaned down. No hurried motion, either. And he took off her pants. He kissed his way back up to her bra and removed it, as well.

Elaina reciprocated, but because the urgency and the heat were taking over her body, she didn't have

Luke's finesse. She practically ripped off his shoulder holster and shirt, and she heard him chuckle.

He was still smiling when he brushed a kiss on the top of her right breast. Then, on the left. He kept going down. Kissing. Her nipples. Her stomach. Her hip. The front of her lacy panties. He used his warm breath and more of those mind-blowing French kisses.

She couldn't catch her breath. And her heart was pounding so hard. The only coherent thought on her mind was for him to take her now. Now. Now. She didn't think she could wait another second.

But Luke made her wait.

He took off her panties with that maddeningly slow pace. He was seducing her, and she was totally helpless to do anything but let it all unfold.

His fingers moved over her. Exploring. Discovering. Pleasuring her. With those same slow strokes that matched an incredibly slow kiss, he eased his fingers inside her. And he found the right spot. Definitely.

The right pace.

And he even had the perfect pressure to make her forget all about the speed that she'd thought she wanted.

Because she could no longer stand, Elaina caught on to him and dropped back onto the bed. They landed in the perfect position, with him between her legs. But his jeans were in the way.

"I want you naked," she warned him.

Elaina found herself fumbling with his zipper. She certainly didn't feel as if she were doing her part to make this work. Then, he kissed her again. It was a reminder of what was waiting for her, and she forgot all about the fumbling. She got the zipper, and managed to rid him of his boots and jeans.

Luke left her for a moment to go get the condom from the bathroom. Each second he was gone seemed like an eternity. By the time he made it back to the bed, Elaina grabbed him and pulled him back down on top of her.

He slid his left hand around the back of her neck and eased his fingers through her hair. By now, she was frantic. Elaina struggled to get what she wanted, but Luke took his time entering her.

It was worth the wait.

Elaina stilled a moment just to savor the sensation of him being inside her. But the stillness didn't last when he began to move. There was no way she could not react to that. Those gentle, deep thrusts were exactly what she wanted.

She wrapped her legs around him to bring them even closer. Luke deepened the closeness with more kisses. It was perfect. But soon, it was no longer enough. Elaina knew this couldn't last. She didn't want it to last. She wanted one thing and that was release.

Luke obviously wanted the same thing. He quickened the pace. So did Elaina. They matched each other. Move for move. Frantic stroke for frantic stroke. Damp skin whispering against damp skin.

Until the pressure built to an unbearable level.

Until the only thing that Elaina could do was go over the edge.

And she took Luke with her.

Chapter Sixteen

Luke quickly came to his senses.

Of course, that didn't happen until he'd taken every bit of pleasure he could possibly take from Elaina.

That made him stupid.

Not because he regretted the sex. Nope. As good as it was, he could never regret that part of it. But he did regret putting her in danger again.

And that's exactly what he'd done.

He certainly hadn't been vigilant despite the fact that less than twenty-four hours earlier, someone had tried to kill them while they were in this very house.

"We need to get dressed," he told her.

He mentally groaned at his tone. It sounded clinical. A real contrast to what had just happened between them. There had been nothing clinical about that. He added a soft kiss on her mouth and hoped it would soften the order he'd just given her.

"We should gather up our things and get them

back to the safe house," he continued. He got up, made a quick trip to the bathroom and returned so he could dress.

Elaina was still on the bed. Naked, of course. She was staring at him as if trying to figure out what he was thinking. He considered reassuring her that all was well. But it would be a lie. All wasn't well. While he'd been having the best sex of his life, the shooter could have gotten past the agent outside and might be ready to go for another round.

And speaking of another round, despite Luke's sated body and urgency to get out of there, he still took the time to admire Elaina. She lay there, her body still damp with sweat. She smelled like sex. And him. It seemed like some kind of primal invitation for him to get back on that bed with her.

But he couldn't.

They'd gotten away with a lapse in judgment, but they might not be so lucky next time.

Elaina finally got up and gathered her clothes. She put on her bra as she went back into the living room to get her shirt. Luke used her absence to check the window to make sure no one was lurking outside. He didn't see anyone, but he still decided to hurry.

Elaina was dressed by the time he walked into the living room. Not only that, she'd gathered up some things—toys and papers—which she obviously wanted to take with her. He strapped on his shoulder holster, picked up his keys and put on his leather jacket.

"Since the other stuff is already in my car in the garage, is there any reason we can't just take it?" she asked.

Normally, the answer would be no since her car could be easily recognized, but since most of Crystal Creek had seen their loaner vehicle in front of the house, there probably was no such thing as a "safe car" for them to use.

"We'll use your car," he agreed.

Elaina walked to the table in the entry. She retrieved her keys, stopped and then fished out a six-inch long jeweler's box that had been shoved to the back of the drawer. "It's a charm bracelet that Kevin gave me. I'd forgotten about it."

Luke took it from her and flipped open the box. The bracelet appeared to be white gold and had six heart charms. He made a cursory examination and decided the hearts were large and thick enough to encase a miniature memory card. "I'll have the lab ultrasound it," he let her know.

She nodded, and they exited through the laundry room. Luke didn't use the remote clipped to her visor to open the garage door until he had the car engine turned on and was ready to drive away. He certainly didn't want to linger around in the open in case that shooter was in the area.

Once they were away from the house, Luke called headquarters to let them know there were en route to the safe house.

"Are we back on the condom issue?" she asked.

Of all the subjects he thought they'd discuss, that wasn't one of them. "Excuse me?"

"The condom that you originally lied about because you didn't want to risk a personal relationship with me. Is this silent, coplike attitude a way of keeping your distance?" But she didn't wait for him to answer. "Because it's not necessary. We can still be friendly—"

"This isn't about you," he interjected.

She studied him a moment, and then her eyes widened. "Oh, God. This is about your late wife, isn't it? I'm so sorry. You're feeling guilty—"

"Wrong again." Though he probably should be feeling guilty. "And *you* have no reason to apologize. I, on the other hand, owe you a huge apology. I should have been watching for the shooter. I should have been doing my job."

"Oh. That." Her look of relief only lasted a few moments before frustration replaced it. "I figured that would come up. The timing wasn't ideal. But we haven't exactly had a lot of opportunities to fall into bed, now have we?"

No. They hadn't. "It happened pretty damn fast."

"That wasn't fast," she muttered, and he could hear the sexual undertones in it.

Or maybe that was his overly active imagination. One thing was for certain, being with Elaina had been memorable.

And distracting.

Even now, he was thinking about her. Well, he was

thinking about having sex with her again, and that was the last thing that should be on his mind. What he should be doing was keeping a close watch on their surroundings.

Luke drove out of town and took the turn onto a rural highway. It definitely wasn't the fastest way to get back to the safe house, nor was it the route they'd used to come to town. He would have to drive well out of their way just to ensure that no one was following them.

His cell phone rang, and Luke fished it out of his jacket pocket. "Agent Buchanan," he answered.

"Agent Roark from headquarters."

Luke recognized the voice. Roark was a fellow agent. Someone he'd worked with on several assignments. He was a good man, and Luke trusted him.

"Are you ready for some good news?" Roark asked.

Luke had braced himself for the worst, but that had him relaxing a bit. "I'd love some."

"We've apprehended one of the escapees, and he's back in custody at Crystal Creek jail."

He experienced both joy and not so much joy. "I'm glad you caught him, but it's probably not a good idea to put him back in the very facility that he managed to escape from."

"It's temporary. We're transporting him to San Antonio this afternoon around two."

The timing was perfect. He could drop Elaina off at the safe house, have lunch with her and Christopher and then go and interrogate this guy.

"I'll see you at two," Luke told him.

"I figured you would."

"They caught the two guys?" Elaina asked the moment he ended the call.

"They caught one of them."

Elaina flattened her hand over her chest as if to steady her heart. "Well, that's one less maniac to worry about."

"It's better than that. During the interrogation, we'll play the one captured off against the one that's still free and make him think that he was sold out by his partner. By this afternoon we could know who these guys really are and who they're working for."

"You really believe that?" she asked.

"Of course. You would, too, if you'd ever seen me in an interrogation room. I'm not usually a screwup, Elaina. I usually do things the right way."

"I didn't mean that. I just didn't want to get my hopes up." She shrugged. "But then, hope is the one thing we have right now."

Unfortunately, it was. "I promise I'll do whatever it takes to end all of this so Christopher and you will be…."

Luke's words trailed off when he glanced in the rearview mirror. The entire time they'd been on country road, he hadn't seen any other vehicles, but there was an SUV coming over the hill behind them. And the driver was going fast.

"What's wrong?" she asked.

"Maybe nothing."

Elaina looked behind them and obviously spotted the SUV. "That driver's getting awfully close to use." Her gaze flew back to him. "What are you thinking?"

He didn't want to say, but this couldn't be good.

Luke drew his weapon so that he'd have easy access, and he sped up. According to the GPS, they had over twenty-eight miles to go before they reached a major intersection. Which meant they were out in the middle of nowhere with this fast-approaching vehicle bearing down on them.

The SUV sped up, as well, and came right up on Luke's bumper. Unfortunately, Luke had to slow down. There was a sharp curve in the road, and just on the other side was a narrow concrete bridge. He couldn't risk hitting that.

But the SUV didn't decrease speed.

"Brace yourself," Luke warned, just as the vehicle rammed them.

The jolt threw his body forward. Elaina's, too. He made a quick check to make sure she was all right, and pressed the emergency button on his phone. That would alert headquarters that he needed assistance, but he didn't want to consider just how long it would take for that assistance to arrive.

Basically, Elaina and he were on their own.

"Can you see the driver?" Elaina asked.

"No." The windows were heavily tinted, and the driver had obviously disengaged the airbag, or it would have popped up during that collision. Too bad it hadn't. It would have slowed him down.

Luke came through the deep curve and approached the bridge. Once he was on the other side, he could speed up.

But he didn't get a chance to do that.

The SUV slammed into them again. Harder this time. And even harder still the third and fourth times.

Luke fought to keep control of his vehicle, but it was a losing battle. The SUV was much bigger, and the driver apparently didn't care if he killed all of them in the process of running them off the road. He didn't have time to think beyond that. The fifth collision caved in the back of the car. He couldn't stop it from happening.

The car went into a skid and flew off the road.

There were no trees or shrubs in their path. Only dirt and rocks. That was the good news. The bad news was that meant there was nothing to break their forward momentum. And, unfortunately, their forward momentum was like an out-of-control roller coaster spearing them straight toward the river.

But it wasn't the river that was the problem.

Because of a drought, the water was hardly more than a stream, but the limestone and clay banks that ravined the river were at least twelve, maybe fifteen, feet high.

If he couldn't stop the car, they would almost certainly plunge to their deaths.

ELAINA SAW THE DEATH trap that lay ahead, and she yelled for Luke to hit the brakes.

But he already had.

Unfortunately, no amount of pressure on the brakes would do any good. The tires couldn't get traction on the silty layers of dirt and pebbles, and they were literally skidding toward that embankment.

She thought of Christopher, praying that she would get to see him again. And she thought of Luke. He was trying so hard to save them, but he might fail.

Elaina tried to brace herself for the inevitable. She didn't have to wait long.

It happened fast.

So fast.

Luke jerked the steering wheel to the right, and the car finally responded. It spun around and came to a stop. A precarious one. Elaina looked out the back window and saw that more than a third of the vehicle was dangling over the stony riverbank.

"Get out!" Luke shouted.

His shout and the wobbling car were all she needed to get moving.

"Hit the ground running," he added. "And head for that cluster of trees."

She spotted the trees. They were at least thirty yards away. And then she realized exactly what he'd said—why he'd told her to hit the ground running. The person responsible for this was up there on the road.

Still, if they stayed in the car, they'd die. The only chance they had was to get to cover.

"Go!" Luke shouted.

She did. Elaina threw open the door and checked to make sure she would land on solid ground. It was close. She barely had room to step out and maneuver around the door.

Her foot slipped, skipping off the winter-damp limestone, but she was determined to survive. She caught on to the door to steady herself.

Once she was certain she wasn't going to plunge to the water and rocks below, she started running. Her adrenaline level was already through the roof, but that sent it soaring even more. She didn't look back. She kept her focus on the trees. She had to get to safety.

Behind her, she heard the crash. The sound of metal crashing into the rock bed.

Her heart went to her knees.

"Luke!" she shouted.

God, had he gotten out of the car before it fell?

Terrified of what she might or might not see, she risked looking back, and Elaina saw him.

Relief flooded through her.

He was there, running toward her, but he also had his gun aimed. His gaze was firing all around them. Probably looking for their attacker. Elaina didn't see the person, but she spotted the SUV on the side of the road just above them.

"Run faster," Luke shouted.

Elaina tried, but the rocky ground beneath her feet didn't exactly cooperate. Just as their car hadn't been able to get traction, neither could she. The nearly freezing air didn't help, either. Her lungs were burning from the near panic and exhaustion, and she couldn't catch her breath. All of that made her feel as if she were moving in slow motion.

Luke remedied the situation. He caught up to her and latched on to her arm. His momentum thrust her forward, and he shoved her into the cover of the trees. He didn't stop there. He put her right against the rough bark of an oak and then sheltered her with his own body.

Elaina tried to level her breathing so she wouldn't make so much noise, but it was impossible. Her lungs were starved for air. Unlike Luke. His breathing was level, and even though he was vigilant, his muscles weren't knotted with tension.

"Do you see anyone?" she whispered in between gasps for breath.

He shook his head.

But someone was out there. The someone that rammed the SUV into their car and nearly gotten them killed.

Who had done this?

Who?

This had to be connected to Kevin and that damn software modification. His stupid antics had nearly gotten her killed—again.

That infuriated her.

For money and greed, he'd left Luke, Christopher and her a legacy of danger.

Luke put his mouth directly against her ear. "I hear footsteps."

She didn't, but then her pulse was pounding so hard that she could hardly hear anything.

He maneuvered her slightly and turned so that his back was to hers. Probably so he could get a better angle to see whom or what was making those footsteps.

But Luke shook his head, and she thought that meant the footsteps had stopped.

Where was this person, this would-be killer? Elaina didn't have to wait long to find out.

A bullet slammed into the tree next to her head.

Chapter Seventeen

Luke pulled Elaina to the ground and dragged her to the other side of the oak. The bullet splintered into the tree, sending debris flying, but he couldn't risk sheltering Elaina with his body.

Because he had to take aim and stop the shooter from firing again.

That bullet had come from behind them, and it'd landed within a fraction of an inch of Elaina's head. It had taken a dozen years off his life to see how close she'd come to dying.

Again, he could blame himself. He shouldn't have allowed this situation to happen. Yet, here they were trapped next to a deep ravine with a shooter behind them. They couldn't jump in the riverbed. That would be nothing short of suicide. Ditto for trying to make it back up the hill to the SUV. That would put them out in the open and in plain sight.

To put it mildly, things looked bad.

A glance down at Elaina confirmed that she knew

the severity of their situation. She looked scared but resolute. His glance confirmed something else that made him irate. There was blood on Elaina's forehead, just above her left eyebrow. It'd probably been caused by a splinter, and it riled him to the core to see her hurt by some cowardly SOB who'd ambushed them.

Luke thanked God that her injury wasn't any worse. At least she was alive. Plus, Elaina and he had one thing on their side. He'd pressed the emergency response button while he was still in the car. Backup was already on the way. Of course, they would have to hold off fire for at least twenty, maybe thirty minutes.

That would no doubt seem like a lifetime.

The next shot confirmed that. Hell. It hadn't come from behind them, but from the front. Specifically, from the side of the SUV.

Luke cursed, grabbed on to Elaina and scrambled for a new position. It was meager at best. The tree wasn't large enough to give them any real cover, and they weren't just dealing with one gunman but two.

The next sound he heard had Luke mentally cursing even more.

Footsteps.

They were crunching on the gravel easement just off the road. By the SUV. But not toward the back of it where the second shot had originated.

Mercy. There were three of them.

He lifted his gun and aimed in the direction of those footsteps. Luke waited.

"I wouldn't do that if were you," a man shouted.

Luke looked to his left, and he saw the guy with the eye patch, the very person who'd tried to kill Elaina and Christopher a year ago.

The anger raged through Luke, but the man was holding a high-powered rifle rigged with a scope. And he had that rifle aimed at Elaina. If Luke tried to shoot now, this bozo would fire right at her. With that scope, he likely wouldn't miss, either.

"Drop your gun," the man said.

"Why, so it'll make it easier for you to shoot us?" was Luke's answer.

"My orders are not to kill you. Yet."

Luke glanced around to make sure no one was sneaking up on them. He couldn't hear footsteps, but that didn't matter. If the trio were armed with rifles, they wouldn't have to get that close to be deadly.

"What do you want?" Elaina yelled.

She was obviously as angry as he was, and that anger came through in her voice. Of course, that anger was slightly diminished by that bloody gash on her forehead.

"You know what we want," the guy told them.

"If I did, I wouldn't have asked."

The man didn't answer immediately. "Your former fiancé was working on a little project. We need the memory disk."

It wasn't a surprise, but knowing the why didn't make it easier for him to figure out how they were going to get out of this alive.

"I don't know where the disk is," Elaina shouted. "If I did, I would have given it to the police."

"Maybe. Maybe not. Kevin had the disk with him when he was at the lawyer's office adopting your son. We know that because Kevin confirmed it."

"To whom?" Luke demanded.

"Me. He trusted me. Obviously that wasn't a wise decision on his part. Anyway, the only place he went after the lawyer's office was to the house in San Antonio that he shared with Elaina."

"And Kevin was killed early that evening when he left to get something from his office," Elaina quickly pointed. "As you well know, since you're the one who probably killed him, I left that night—after you tried to kill me."

He didn't deny it. He just stood there with that rifle pointed down at her. "But you took things with you when you ran. That memory disk had to be in those things because it wasn't in the house. We checked."

Elaina started to answer, but Luke nudged her to keep her quiet. He could go two ways with this. He could refuse to tell the man anything else, or he could tell him the truth and hope that it would disperse the three so that Luke would have a better chance at picking them off one by one.

Luke went with the second option.

"Those things that Elaina took with her from the house? Well, they're in the car," Luke informed him. "Thanks to you, those things are now in the river. If they haven't been destroyed by the crash or the water, they probably won't last long. In fact, they might be floating away at this very moment."

That got a reaction. The man lifted his head and looked in the direction of the SUV. He was probably waiting for his comrade or boss to tell him what to do. He must have gotten some kind of signal because he nodded toward the gunman who was behind Luke.

That minor distraction was all Luke needed. He shoved Elaina face-first onto the ground, he aimed, and he fired at the man with the eye patch. One shot to the head was all it took, and the man crumpled into a heap.

Luke didn't stop there. Staying low, he rotated his body and took aim at the gunman behind them.

But it was too late.

The man had already stood and had his rifle targeted right at them. He looked as if he knew what he was doing, and Luke didn't doubt that the guy was a pro. A hired gun. Dressed head to toe in winter camouflaged hunting clothes that explained why Luke hadn't been able to spot him earlier.

"My advice?" the guy snarled. "Don't move."

Luke didn't, mainly because he couldn't risk getting killed. If this goon eliminated him, then Elaina stood little to no chance of making it out of there. Worse, they might be able to drug her so that she'd tell them the location of the safe house. They might go there to search for the disk and create God knows what kind of dangerous havoc. Christopher could be in danger.

And that wasn't going to happen.

The gunman tilted his head slightly and mumbled something. Luke realized he wasn't speaking to them but to a tiny grape-size communicator on the collar of his hunting jacket.

"What's happening?" Elaina asked.

Luke knew she couldn't see since her face was practically right in the dirt, but he wasn't so sure it would do her any good to witness that big guy aiming another rifle at him. And the gunman seemed a little riled that Luke had killed his comrade.

"It's a standoff," Luke told Elaina.

"Not quite," the gunman countered.

Luke wasn't sure what he meant by that, but then he heard the footsteps again. They were coming from the direction of the SUV.

"The boss will keep an eye on you," the gunman explained in such a fake cheerful voice that Luke wanted to slug him for that alone. "While I search the car. For your sake, that disk had better be there."

"Why, so you can kill us anyway?" Luke challenged while he kept his ear tuned to those footsteps.

He needed to keep this situation under control until backup arrived. Control, in this case, likely meant being held at gunpoint by the "boss" while the goon went down into that ravine. Luke liked those odds—him against the idiot responsible for all of this.

Because Luke needed a back-up plan, he had to put Elaina in a position to evade and escape. He eased away from her. She immediately sat up and looked around. From the corner of his eye, he could tell that she was looking at him. Probably for answers about what they were going to do next but he couldn't risk taking his attention off the gunman. After all, the man didn't need Elaina and him alive to do the search.

The footsteps stopped just a few yards away, and the gunman hurried toward the creek.

Luke shifted toward the newcomer, knowing he was about to come face-to-face with the person who'd already attempted to kill them. There would likely be another attempt within the next couple of minutes.

"Agent Buchanan, Elaina," the woman greeted them. "I'd hoped it wouldn't come to this. Drop the gun, or I'll shoot Elaina."

Elaina lifted her head. Luke did, as well, and he speared the woman's gaze.

He found himself looking down the barrel of an assault rifle.

And the woman behind the trigger was Brenda McQueen.

ELAINA HADN'T KNOWN exactly whom she would see holding that rifle on them, but she wasn't surprised to see Brenda. After all, the woman was one of their main suspects.

"Drop the gun," Brenda ordered Luke. "Or Elaina dies, right here, right now. You might not be her real husband, but I don't think you want her blood on your hands."

Elaina held her breath. Waiting. Luke had probably

been trained not to surrender her weapon. Plus, if he was unarmed, it would make them both targets.

"If she kills me," Elaina said to him. "Then you'll just shoot her. That way, one of us will be around to raise Christopher."

"Oh, that's so touching," Brenda mocked. "But Agent Buchanan cares for you. He can't let you die. He's too honorable to do something like that."

"Let me die," Elaina whispered.

But he didn't. And Brenda was right—there was no way that Luke would stand there and watch her die.

Luke lowered the gun and eased it onto the ground in front of them. Brenda didn't waste any time, she kicked it out of his reach.

"You have to know where that disk is," Brenda challenged, and she directed that challenge at Elaina.

"Kevin kept a lot of things secret. The only thing he ever said about the project was that he was working for someone named T."

"That's old news," Brenda insisted. "I'm T. And I paid that weasel fiancé of yours a lot of money that investors had given me. Kevin didn't deliver, and now I've got those investors breathing down my neck."

"Don't expect us to feel sorry for you," Luke snarled.

"Well, you should. That memory disk is nothing to you, but I'm within a week of being murdered if I don't produce it. Believe me, my investors are not the sympathetic type, and I'm going to deliver that disk." She turned back to Elaina. "Think back to the night Kevin brought the baby home. What did he have with him?"

"You really expect me to help you?" Elaina asked.

"If you want to live, you will."

Elaina shrugged. "You're planning to kill us no matter what I say."

Brenda readjusted her aim. The rifle was no longer aimed at Elaina.

But Luke.

"Talk, cooperate," Brenda ordered. "Or I kill Agent Buchanan."

"Go ahead," Luke offered.

But Elaina knew from the moment Brenda had made her threat that the woman would indeed carry it out. And just as Luke couldn't let her die, Elaina couldn't let that happen to him.

"See what happens when you get involved with someone," Brenda commented. "You let your heart and other body parts do your thinking."

Elaina didn't necessarily consider that an insult.

"Well?" Brenda prompted. "What did dear ol' Kevin have with him that night?"

Elaina could either lie or tell the truth. She went with the truth because she hoped that if she named an item that might have the disk, then Brenda would have to go after it. She likely wouldn't attempt to kill them until she was sure she had what she wanted.

"Kevin brought home the baby and the adoption papers," Elaina answered. "Christopher was in a carrier seat, and he was wrapped in a blue blanket. He wore a gown with a drawstring at the bottom and a knit cap with a little pom-pom on top. All of that is in the car. He also had a pacifier, a bottle and some disposable diapers. They aren't in the car. I didn't keep them."

"Then you'd better hope that the memory disk is in one of the things you did keep. Because, you see, Elaina, I can make your deaths very quick and easy. Or I can decide not to do that."

Elaina looked at Luke to see how he was handling those threats, but he had a poker face. Well, except for the slight lift of his right eyebrow. She didn't know what it meant exactly, but Elaina figured he was about to do something. She only hoped that something didn't get him killed.

"Backup will be here soon," Luke informed Brenda.

"Yes. I assumed that you'd contacted them. We've got fifteen, maybe twenty minutes." She glanced down at her watch.

Luke moved so quickly that it was practically a blur. He launched himself at the woman.

Just as Brenda fired the rifle at Elaina.

Chapter Eighteen

Luke tried not to let Brenda's shot distract him. He tried to keep his attention aimed on tackling and disarming her. But he couldn't stayed totally focused.

Because that bullet could have hit Elaina.

Hell, it could have killed her.

He aimed all his fear, rage and adrenaline at Brenda. He plowed into her, all the while listening for any sound that Elaina had been hurt. But all he could hear was Brenda.

Yelling and screaming at him, Brenda fought him, hard, and she was much stronger than Luke had anticipated. Still, he outsized her, and he had a more powerful motive for winning—Elaina. He had to get to her in case she needed medical attention. The only way for that to happen was for him to neutralize Brenda.

Luke used his body weight and sheer strength to put Brenda in a chokehold. He kicked the rifle from her hands and rotated both their bodies so that he could see what was going on with Elaina.

She was still there, by the tree, but the sleeve of her jacket had been gashed open, and he could see the blood. His worst fear were confirmed.

Elaina had been shot.

Her injury didn't stop her from moving though. Wincing and holding her arm, she hurried to gather up both the rifle and his handgun. She managed to get the first but not the second when Luke heard the man's voice.

"Hold it right there."

It was the camouflaged gunman. He'd obviously climbed out of the riverbed when he heard his boss call for help. The man had dropped the boxes of items he'd taken from their car, and he was now holding a gun on Elaina.

"Don't," Luke warned her when Elaina started to aim the rifle at the man. It would be suicide. The guy was already cocked and loaded, and Luke figured a hired gun wouldn't miss. Elaina, however, had no experience with weapons.

"Let Brenda go," the man told Luke.

Hell. They were right back where they started, except this time it was worse because of Elaina's injury.

"How badly are you hurt?" he asked while he still kept a chokehold on Brenda.

"I'll live," she said. "I promise."

It was a promise that Luke knew she couldn't keep unless he could get her to a hospital right away. She was losing way too much blood.

"Let go of me!" Brenda yelled.

She rammed her elbow into Luke's stomach, and because of the rifle pointed at Elaina, he knew he'd have no choice but to let her go—eventually.

Still, he had to do something. The gunman had the things from the car. That was everything that Brenda and he needed, which meant they were likely going to be killed now.

Luke couldn't let that happen.

He came up with a quick plan. It wasn't a good one, and it had nearly as many risks as just standing there and facing down these SOBs. He took a deep breath, said a quick prayer and he let go of Brenda.

Cursing and hitting him, the woman struggled to get to her feet. Luke waited until Brenda stood before he made his next move.

"Drop to the ground!" he shouted to Elaina.

Thank God she listened. Elaina dove in the direction of his gun, and he hooked his leg around Brenda's. As he'd known it would do, it off-balanced her, and Brenda came crashing right back into his arms.

With the position of their bodies, the gunman wouldn't have a clean shot for either Elaina or him, unless the guy planned to risk hitting his boss.

Luke tried to move fast, and while he was doing it, he tried to gain control of the howling, fighting woman who obviously wasn't going to cooperate with his plan. He managed to put her back in a choke-hold, and he dragged her in front of him to act as a shield. He didn't stop there. He moved both of them in front of Elaina so he could protect her.

His plan had worked, but he figured it would work even better when he heard something he'd been praying to hear.

A siren.

Backup was about to arrive. Still, from the sound of it, help could be several minutes out.

Too much could still happen.

"I'm not going to jail," the gunman informed them. And the man did something that Luke had not anticipated.

He aimed his rifle at Brenda.

"What do you think you're doing?" Brenda yelled.

"Investing in my future. This way, if the memory disk is in these things, I'll find it and market it on my own."

Brenda cursed at him, and it wasn't mild. She continued to call him names while she struggled and kicked to get out of Luke's grip.

Luke faced a new dilemma. It was obvious the gunman would kill his boss if Luke continued to hold her in place. However, if he let Brenda go, then the guy would just shoot Elaina and him. What Luke needed was his gun. That would give him a chance to fight back.

The gunman made a sudden shift of motion. He angled his body away from Brenda.

And took aim at Elaina.

Luke looked down at her and saw that Elaina had not only moved out of cover to retrieve his gun, she'd pointed it at the man. Her hand was shaking, maybe because she was afraid, but he knew she could also be going into shock.

"Don't!" Luke yelled, hoping to draw the gunman's attention back to him.

When that didn't work, when it seemed as if they were seconds away from a shootout—a shootout that Elaina probably couldn't win—Luke had to take drastic action.

"Elaina, don't shoot," he whispered.

And he hoped like the devil that she'd heard him.

Luke shoved Brenda to the side, in front of Elaina, so that he could try to protect her. In the same motion, Luke snatched the gun from her hand. He took aim at the man.

He fired.

And fired.

And fired.

The man didn't go down. Even though Luke knew he'd delivered direct hits to the gunman's torso and chest. The seconds seemed to tick away, and the entire woods were quiet except their breathing and the howl of the approaching siren. Finally, the gunman fell to the ground.

Brenda immediately kicked Luke and went for her rifle. She might have succeeded if both Elaina and he hadn't dove at the woman. Both landed hard against Brenda, and all of them fell into a heap.

The impact knocked Luke's gun from his hands.

It was a race to see who would get it first, and while Luke fought to retrieve it, he was also mindful of Elaina. He didn't want to risk further injuring her, but he couldn't risk Brenda getting the gun, either. There was just enough time for her to kill them and try to escape.

Luke made sure that didn't happen.

He grabbed on to the back of Brenda's neck and shoved her against the ground. He anchored her in place with the upper half of his body and kicked the rifle toward Elaina. She grabbed it and then handed him his gun.

"Give me a reason to kill you," Luke snarled to Brenda as he put his gun against her head. "Any reason."

Just like that Brenda stopped struggling. But she didn't stop cursing. Luke didn't mind the profanity. He could handle anything as long as he knew Elaina was safe.

But was she safe?

She was pale and trembling, and her entire arm was now soaked with blood.

"I think I'm okay," Elaina assured him with her voice shaking as much as body.

It wasn't much of an assurance, and Luke knew she probably wouldn't stay conscious for long. He needed to get her to the hospital immediately.

A sheriff's car screeched to a halt right behind the SUV. Two men barreled out of the vehicle. Both were armed and ready. One was Sheriff Dawson, and Luke recognized the other as Agent Simon Roark.

"We're down here," Luke called out to them.

Luke didn't waste any time. As soon as the sheriff and Agent Roark got to them, he passed Brenda off to them, and he went to Elaina. Behind him, he heard the agent call for an ambulance. Good. Because they were going to need one.

He pulled Elaina to him so that he could keep her warm and because he desperately needed to hold her.

"I'm sorry about this," he whispered. He checked her wound, but there was so much blood, he couldn't tell just how bad it was.

"Why *are* you sorry?" she asked, blinking.

"Because I should be the one hurt and bleeding. Not you."

She managed a weak smile, but it faded as quickly as it came. "If I don't make it—"

"An ambulance is on the way," he said. He didn't want to hear this.

Elaina apparently thought he should hear it. "Yes. But if something goes wrong—"

"It won't."

She huffed, but it, too, was weak and filled with breath. "You need to let me finish."

"I know what you're going to say. That if something goes wrong, you want me to take care of Christopher. You know I will. But nothing will go wrong. It can't."

She shook her head, reached up and touched his face with her fingertips. Her hands were as cold as death.

"Things don't always work out for the best," Elaina muttered. Her eyelids eased down.

"Both of us have firsthand knowledge of that.

That's why it'll work this time," Luke promised. "It has to work. Because I won't lose you. Understand? I won't lose you."

But he was talking to himself.

Elaina was no longer conscious.

LUKE PACED. He sat down. Got up. And paced some more. None of that helped. He wasn't sure how much more he could take of this. He had to know what was going on in that E.R. procedure room where the doctor was with Elaina.

"These exams take time," Agent Roark commented. His fellow agent had followed the ambulance to the Luling Rehabilitation Hospital and was now sorting through the box of Elaina's items that they'd retrieved from the riverbank.

Luke glared at Roark for that totally unhelpful observation. Of course, these things took time. The doctor had already been in there a half hour.

It'd seemed like a decade.

Roark checked his watch. "The sitter and Christopher should be here soon."

Yes. Theresa and Christopher were indeed on their way from the safe house to the hospital. Luke prayed there'd be good news about Elaina before they arrived.

"You know, you could get your mind off things if you helped me go through these things," Roark continued.

Luke glanced at the items the agent had placed on the table of the private waiting room. The last thing he wanted to do was work, but if he didn't do something, *anything,* he might have to put his fist through the wall.

Once again, he'd nearly gotten Elaina killed.

He refused to believe that she could die. She couldn't. Somehow, she had to make it through this. Then he could tell her how sorry he was. Maybe, just maybe, she'd forgive him.

Or maybe she'd order him out of her life.

He couldn't blame her if she did.

"I don't see anything in this charm bracelet that could hold a disk," Roark informed him.

Luke was of the same opinion, but that miniature memory disk had to be somewhere. And he still needed to find it. Luke wanted Brenda and those investors out of Elaina and Christopher's lives. He darn sure didn't want these goons showing up in the near future to make a second attempt at finding the disk. So, that meant he had to find it and get it as far away from Elaina and Christopher as he could.

Drawing in a long breath, Luke sank down into the metal fold-up chair across the table from Roark. Luke stared at the items and tried to put himself in Kevin's place. Kevin, a sleazy liar on the verge of becoming a rich, big-time criminal. Yet, in the middle of that big software modification venture, he'd illegally adopted Christopher.

A coincidence?

Luke didn't believe in them, especially when it came to criminal behavior.

He picked up the clothes that his son had worn on

the trip from the lawyer's office to Elaina and Kevin's home. A soft knitted cap with a tiny pom-pom on top. A long gown with a drawstring. And a blanket rimmed with satin. All in varying shades of blue.

Luke moved those three items, the denim infant carrier seat and the adoption papers to one end of the table. He added the purple stuffed bear and yellow bunny. He remembered that Elaina had said that Kevin had called Christopher their little bunny. Kevin's pet name still didn't sit well with Luke. But unless the memory disk was in the items that Elaina had already discarded, like the pacifier and bottle, then it was likely here.

So, where would Kevin have hidden it?

Luke mentally went back to that night, and he tried to imagine what Kevin would have been feeling. The excitement mixed with a hefty dose of caution. Maybe even fear. Maybe he even knew that there were killers after him.

Where was the one place Kevin would hide the tiny disk? A disk that could cost him his life or else give him the life he'd always wanted?

And suddenly Luke knew the answer.

Chapter Nineteen

"I'm feeling great," Elaina insisted as the nurse wrapped her freshly stitched wound. She looked at the doctor to continue her plea for freedom. "Really great, considering everything that's happened. I'm ready to leave the hospital."

The doctor with the craggy face, Roman nose and sugar-white hair made a sound that could have meant anything or nothing, and he wrote something down on her chart. But Elaina knew the truth. Her arm had been wounded, and the adrenaline crash was making her feel bone-tired. The pain meds had made her a little woozy. But she wasn't critical. Heck, she wasn't even in serious condition.

But Luke didn't know that yet.

He was probably out in the waiting room blaming himself for all of this. She needed to set him straight before his guilt built to massive portions. And she also needed to feel his arms around her. While she was wishing and needing, she added Christopher to the list. She wanted to see her baby.

"You can't leave the hospital just yet," the doctor informed her. "You'll stay the night for observation, and then you'll have to come back to have those stitches checked."

Elaina barely heard him. She had only one thing on her mind. "I want to see Luke."

"So you've said at least a dozen times." The doctor examined the bandage when the nurse moved away. "He's asked at least that many times, too. Oh, and someone named Carrie keeps calling the nurses' station."

Elaina would talk to her later and tell her she wouldn't be returning to Crystal Creek. Once she'd recovered, she'd look for a place closer to Luke so that both of them would be able to see Christopher.

Well, she would do that if Luke approved. She had to get past that obstacle first.

"I want to see Luke," Elaina repeated.

He nodded. "Let me do something about fulfilling that request." The doctor left the room and walked across the hall. The nurse followed him.

Elaina couldn't hear what the doctor said, but she heard Luke. He came rushing into the room and came to a halt next to her bed. He looked rumpled, exhausted and worried. But he also looked incredibly hot. Of course, looking hot was the norm for Luke Buchanan.

"How are you?" he asked.

She told him what the doctor had told her when he made his initial examination. "I'll be all right.

The bullet went straight through and didn't damage any nerves."

Luke didn't take her word for it. He sank down onto the edge of the bed and examined her bandaged arm. And then her eyes. She examined his eyes, too. Yep, there was a hefty amount of guilt mixed with the fatigue.

Elaina decided to nip this in the bud. "You're not responsible for this."

He groaned. "Oh, yes, I am."

She shook her head and touched his hand. "Let's give ourselves a break and blame Brenda and Kevin."

Luke looked ready to argue with that, so Elaina leaned over and kissed him. He cooperated. Luke slipped his arms around her, eased her to him and returned the kiss.

It was heaven.

He was warm and solid, and he gave her exactly what she needed—*him*. But it didn't last nearly long enough.

Luke pulled back and met her gaze. "I do have some good news. I found the memory disk, and it's already on the way to crime lab."

Well, she certainly hadn't expected that news. But it, too, was like heaven. Hallelujah! They were free from Kevin's horrible legacy.

"Where did you find it?" Elaina asked.

"Behind the raised gold seal on the adoption papers. The seal was thick and nearly two inches wide, and I guess that's why no one noticed that anything was hidden beneath it. I figured that a fake adoption meant fake papers. Kevin wouldn't have wanted to put the tiny disk where it would be handled or crushed. He knew the papers would be kept in a file, waiting for him to retrieve it whenever he needed it."

Of course. She only wished she'd thought of that sooner. "Maybe the crime lab will be able to tell us why Brenda wanted that disk so badly."

"The lead investigators think they know. It appears Kevin was trying to implant complex computer viruses into commonly used antiviral software. These viruses would basically destroy a computer network's firewall and security measures. And it was aimed at banks and credit card institutions. Software like that could have made billons for anyone breaking into those cyber accounts."

Elaina had to take a moment to absorb that. "Billons," she whispered. No wonder Brenda had been willing to kill to get her hands on it.

"What about Carrie?" Elaina wanted to know. "She wasn't involved with this, was she?"

"No. It doesn't look like it."

"So, we're safe now?" Elaina asked.

Luke nodded. Then, shrugged. "Well, safe from bad guys. We still have some personal things to deal with. First of all, I want you to slap me for nearly getting you killed."

She huffed. She'd rather set her hair on fire than hit him. "I said we weren't going to do this. You're not to blame. Truth is, you saved me. Not just my life." She had to clear the lump in her throat before she could continue. "You saved *me*."

He didn't say anything. He sat there, staring at her. And that suddenly made Elaina feel uncomfortable. Had her confession of the heart been too much for him to handle?

"You still don't think I'm faking my feelings?" she asked hesitantly.

Luke blinked. "No. God, no."

Whew. That was something, but it didn't explain the change in mood. "Then why the glum face?"

He, too, cleared his throat. Not once. But twice. And he scratched his forehead. "Because I have something to say, to *suggest,*" he corrected. "And I'm not sure how you're going to take it."

Oh. This was about Christopher's custody. That sapped what little energy she had left, and she eased her head back onto the pillow. "Go ahead," she prompted.

"You're exhausted. We can talk about this another time," Luke said. He started to stand, but she caught on to his arm.

"No. Let's get this out into the open."

He waited, looking at her, probably to make sure she was up to this.

"Go ahead," Elaina repeated. "Just please tell me that you'll give me visitation rights with Christopher."

Another blink, and he stared at her as if she'd lost her mind. "Visitation rights? That's what you want?" But he didn't wait for her to answer. "Because I want something more than that."

Since he wasn't smiling and since his intensity level was through the roof, Elaina had no idea where this was going.

"We could do this the safe way," he continued after clearing his throat. "We could spend the next year or so getting to know each other, to make sure that we're ready for a relationship."

She mentally repeated that and tried not to jump for joy. Her stitches couldn't handle that, even if that's what her heart begged her to do. "You want a relationship with me?"

He shook his head.

Her heart went into a nosedive. "The blood loss must have left me with a foggy head, because I'm confused."

He leaned in and kissed her, making her even more confused and foggy headed. He also left her breathless, incredibly warm and wanting more of him.

"Not just a relationship," he clarified. "I want to make love to you."

Oh, that remedied her nosediving heart. Elaina smiled and felt herself go all warm. "I think that can be arranged. Not now. Not here. But soon."

He smiled, too, and it made it all the way to his eyes. "I was thinking of lots of sex. On a regular basis. With us under the same roof."

Elaina was sure her smile widened to a ridiculous proportion. "I'd like that, to be under the same roof with you and Christopher."

But then, her smile faded.

She hated to say this. She truly did. But it had to be said. "I don't want a relationship of convenience."

He shrugged. "Trust me, being married to me will be anything but convenient. I'm pigheaded, moody and often a pain in the butt."

This time, her heart nearly stopped. "Married?"

Luke pulled away from her, went down on one knee and took her hand. "Let me back up a little. Will you marry me?"

She couldn't breathe. Couldn't answer. Couldn't move. Elaina just sat there with her mouth open.

"Please," Luke whispered. "Don't say no."

She tried to speak, but her mouth didn't cooperate. How had this happened? One day she was living a lie, and now she had the real possibility of living a real life. With Luke and Christopher.

"I love you," she heard Luke say. "I realized that when I nearly lost you."

Oh, mercy. That's when she'd realized she loved him. The tears came. Happy tears.

Luke stood. "Is that a no?"

She shook her head. "No."

He looked as if she'd slugged him.

"I don't mean no as in no to your proposal," she quickly clarified. "I mean no, I don't mean a no."

"Is, uh, that your way of saying yes, you'll marry me?" he asked.

Elaina didn't trust her mouth or her brain to answer him so she latched on to him and pulled her to him. Her injury protested the exertion, but she ignored the pain. She ignored everything but Luke. She kissed him, and she hoped that everything she felt for him came through in that kiss.

Luke turned the tables on her though. He kissed her, too. Mercy, he really did love her.

"I love you, too," she managed to say.

He nodded, and there were tears in his eyes. Elaina was past that point. Her tears were streaming down her cheeks. She'd never felt happier or more complete.

But it suddenly got a lot better.

She heard the babbling noises in the hall, and both Luke and she turned in that direction. A moment later, Theresa appeared in the doorway. She was holding Christopher in her arms.

"See," Theresa said pointing to Elaina and Luke. "I told you that Ma Ma and Da Da were here."

Christopher eyed them, especially the hospital bed and Elaina's bandaged arm. Then, he smiled and reached out for Luke to take him.

Luke did. He took Christopher, kissed his cheek and walked to Elaina so that she could kiss him, as well.

Elaina slid her arm around both of her guys. Christopher tolerated the hugs and kisses for a few moments and then wiggled out of her embrace. He babbled something that she couldn't distinguish. Something happy, no doubt, since he giggled and patted Luke on the cheek.

"Ma Ma, Da Da," Christopher said.

And this time, it was crystal clear.

Elaina's feelings were crystal clear, as well. In fact, she'd never been more certain.

"Yes," she told Luke.

He whipped around to face her. "Yes to what?"

"To everything. Yes, to being your wife. Yes, to us being a family."

He nodded. Kissed her until she couldn't breathe. Then, he gathered both Christopher and her into his arms and held on tight.

* * * * *

Look for more books in Delores Fossen's brand-new miniseries, FIVE-ALARM BABIES, *later this year from Harlequin Intrigue.*

Mediterranean Nights

Join the guests and crew of **Alexandra's Dream**, *the newest luxury ship to set sail on the romantic Mediterranean, as they experience the glamorous world of cruising.*

A new Harlequin continuity series begins in June 2007 with *FROM RUSSIA, WITH LOVE* *by Ingrid Weaver*

Marina Artamova books a cabin on the luxurious cruise ship **Alexandra's Dream**, *when she finds out that her orphaned nephew and his adoptive father are aboard. She's determined to be reunited with the boy…but the romantic ambience of the ship and her undeniable attraction to a man she considers her enemy are about to interfere with her quest!*

Turn the page for a sneak preview!

Piraeus, Greece

"THERE SHE IS, Stefan. *Alexandra's Dream*." David Anderson squatted beside his new son and pointed at the dark blue hull that towered above the pier. The cruise ship was a majestic sight, twelve decks high and as long as a city block. A circle of silver and gold stars, the logo of the Liberty Cruise Line, gleamed from the swept-back smokestack. Like some legendary sea creature born for the water, the ship emanated power from every sleek curve—even at rest it held the promise of motion. "That's going to be our home for the next ten days."

The child beside him remained silent, his cheeks working in and out as he sucked furiously on his thumb. Hair so blond it appeared white ruffled against his forehead in the harbor breeze. The baby-sweet scent unique to the very young mingled with the tang of the sea.

"Ship," David said. "Uh, *parakhod*."

From beneath his bangs, Stefan looked at the *Alexandra's Dream*. Although he didn't release his thumb, the corners of his mouth tightened with the beginning of a smile.

David grinned. That was Stefan's first smile this afternoon, one of only two since they had left the orphanage yesterday. It was probably because of the boat—according to the orphanage staff, the boy loved boats, which was the main reason David had decided to book this cruise. Then again, there was a strong possibility the smile could have been a reaction to David's attempt at pocket-dictionary Russian. Whatever the cause, it was a good start.

The liaison from the adoption agency had claimed that Stefan had been taught some English, but David had yet to see evidence of it. David continued to speak, positive his son would understand his tone even if he couldn't grasp the words. "This is her maiden voyage. Her first trip, just like this is our first trip, and that makes it special." He motioned toward the stage that had been set up on the pier beneath the ship's bow. "That's why everyone's celebrating."

The ship's official christening ceremony had been held the day before and had been a closed affair, with only the cruise-line executives and VIP guests invited, but the stage hadn't yet been disassembled. Banners bearing the blue and white of the Greek flag of the ship's owner, as well as the Liberty circle of stars logo, draped the edges of the platform. In the center, a group of musicians and a dance troupe dressed in traditional white folk costumes performed for the benefit of the *Alexandra's Dream*'s first passengers. Their audience was in a festive mood, snapping their fingers in time to the music while the dancers twirled and wove through their steps.

David bobbed his head to the rhythm of the mandolins. They were playing a folk tune that seemed vaguely familiar, possibly from a movie he'd seen. He hummed a few notes. "Catchy melody, isn't it?"

Stefan turned his gaze on David. His eyes were a striking shade of blue, as cool and pale as a winter horizon and far too solemn for a child not yet five. Still, the smile that hovered at the corners of his mouth persisted. He moved his head with the music, mirroring David's motion.

David gave a silent cheer at the interaction. Hopefully, this cruise would provide countless opportunities for more. "Hey, good for you," he said. "Do you like the music?"

The child's eyes sparked. He withdrew his thumb with a pop. *"Moozika!"*

"Music. Right!" David held out his hand. "Come on, let's go closer so we can watch the dancers."

Stefan grasped David's hand quickly, as if he feared it would be withdrawn. In an instant his budding smile was replaced by a look close to panic.

Did he remember the car accident that had killed his parents? It would be a mercy if he didn't. As far as David knew, Stefan had never spoken of it to anyone. Whatever he had seen had made him run so far from the crash that the police hadn't found him until the next day. The event had traumatized him to the extent that he hadn't uttered a word until his fifth week at the orphanage. Even now he seldom talked.

David sat back on his heels and brushed the hair from Stefan's forehead. That solemn, too-old gaze locked with his, and for an instant, David felt as if he looked back in time at an image of himself thirty years ago.

He didn't need to speak the same language to understand exactly how this boy felt. He knew what it meant to be alone and powerless among strangers, trying to be brave and tough but wishing with every fiber of his being for a place to belong, to be safe, and most of all for someone to love him....

He knew in his heart he would be a good parent to Stefan. It was why he had never considered halting the adoption process after Ellie had left him. He hadn't balked when he'd learned of the recent claim by Stefan's spinster aunt, either; the absentee relative had shown up too late for her case to be considered. The adoption was meant to be. He and this child already shared a bond that went deeper than paper-work or legalities.

A seagull screeched overhead, making Stefan start and press closer to David.

"That's my boy," David murmured. He swallowed hard, struck by the simple truth of what he had just said.

That's my *boy*.

"I CAN'T BE PATIENT, RUDOLPH. I'm not going to stand by and watch my nephew get ripped from his country and his roots to live on the other side of the world."

Rudolph hissed out a slow breath. "Marina, I don't like the sound of that. What are you planning?"

"I'm going to talk some sense into this American kidnapper."

"No. Absolutely not. No offence, but diplomacy is not your strong suit."

"Diplomacy be damned. Their ship's due to sail at five o'clock."

"Then you wouldn't have an opportunity to speak with him even if his lawyer agreed to a meeting."

"I'll have ten days of opportunities, Rudolph, since I plan to be on board that ship."

* * * * *

*Follow Marina and David as they join forces
to uncover the reason behind little Stefan's
unusual silence, and the secret behind
the death of his parents....*

Look for From Russia, With Love
*by Ingrid Weaver
in stores June 2007.*

Mediterranean N I G H T S™

Tycoon Elias Stamos is launching his newest luxury cruise ship from his home port in Greece. But someone from his past is eager to expose old secrets and to see the Stamos empire crumble.

Mediterranean Nights
launches in June 2007 with...

FROM RUSSIA, WITH LOVE
by *Ingrid Weaver*

Join the guests and crew of *Alexandra's Dream* as they are drawn into a world of glamour, romance and intrigue in this new 12-book series.

www.eHarlequin.com

MN1

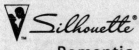
Silhouette®

Romantic
SUSPENSE

Sparked *by* **Danger,**
Fueled *by* **Passion.**

This month and every month look for
four new heart-racing romances
set against a backdrop of suspense!

Available in June 2007

Shelter from the Storm
by RaeAnne Thayne

A Little Bit Guilty
(Midnight Secrets miniseries)
by Jenna Mills

Mob Mistress
by Sheri WhiteFeather

A Serial Affair
by Natalie Dunbar

Available wherever you buy books!

Visit Silhouette Books at www.eHarlequin.com   SRS0507

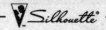

SPECIAL EDITION™

COMING IN JUNE

HER LAST
FIRST DATE

by *USA TODAY* bestsellling author
SUSAN MALLERY

After one too many bad dates, Crissy Phillips
finally swore off men. Recently widowed,
pediatrician Josh Daniels can't risk losing his
heart. With an intense attraction pulling them
together, will their fear keep them apart?
Or will one wild night change everything...?

**Sometimes the unexpected
is the best news of all....**

Visit Silhouette Books at www.eHarlequin.com SSE24831

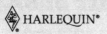

HARLEQUIN®

INTRIGUE®

ARE YOU AFRAID OF THE DARK?

The eerie text message was only part of a night to
remember for security ace Shane Peters—one minute
he was dancing with Princess Ariana LeBron, holding
her in his arms at a soiree of world leaders, the next he
was fighting for their lives when a blackout struck and
gunmen held them hostage. Their demands were simple:
give them the princess.

Part of a new miniseries:

LIGHTS OUT

ROYAL LOCKDOWN

BY RUTH GLICK

WRITING AS
REBECCA YORK

On sale June 2007.

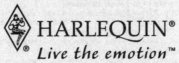

HARLEQUIN®
Live the emotion™

www.eHarlequin.com   HIMAY07

REQUEST YOUR FREE BOOKS!

2 FREE NOVELS PLUS 2 FREE GIFTS!

HARLEQUIN®

INTRIGUE®

Breathtaking Romantic Suspense

YES! Please send me 2 FREE Harlequin Intrigue® novels and my 2 FREE gifts. After receiving them, if I don't wish to receive any more books, I can return the shipping statement marked "cancel." If I don't cancel, I will receive 6 brand-new novels every month and be billed just $4.24 per book in the U.S., or $4.99 per book in Canada, plus 25¢ shipping and handling per book and applicable taxes, if any*. That's a savings of close to 15% off the cover price! I understand that accepting the 2 free books and gifts places me under no obligation to buy anything. I can always return a shipment and cancel at any time. Even if I never buy another book from Harlequin, the two free books and gifts are mine to keep forever.

182 HDN EEZ7 382 HDN EEZK

Name	(PLEASE PRINT)	
Address		Apt. #
City	State/Prov.	Zip/Postal Code

Signature (if under 18, a parent or guardian must sign)

Mail to the **Harlequin Reader Service®**:
IN U.S.A.: P.O. Box 1867, Buffalo, NY 14240-1867
IN CANADA: P.O. Box 609, Fort Erie, Ontario L2A 5X3

Not valid to current Harlequin Intrigue subscribers.

Want to try two free books from another line?

Call 1-800-873-8635 or visit www.morefreebooks.com.

* Terms and prices subject to change without notice. NY residents add applicable sales tax. Canadian residents will be charged applicable provincial taxes and GST. This offer is limited to one order per household. All orders subject to approval. Credit or debit balances in a customer's account(s) may be offset by any other outstanding balance owed by or to the customer. Please allow 4 to 6 weeks for delivery.

Your Privacy: Harlequin is committed to protecting your privacy. Our Privacy Policy is available online at www.eHarlequin.com or upon request from the Reader Service. From time to time we make our lists of customers available to reputable firms who may have a product or service of interest to you. If you would prefer we not share your name and address, please check here. ☐

HI07

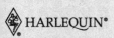

HARLEQUIN®

American ROMANCE®

**is proud to present a special treat this
Fourth of July with three stories
to kick off your summer!**

SUMMER LOVIN'
by
**Marin Thomas,
Laura Marie Altom
Ann Roth**

This year, celebrating the Fourth of July in Silver Cliff,
Colorado, is going to be special. There's an all-year
high school reunion taking place before the old
school building gets torn down. As old flames find
each other and new romances begin, this small
town is looking like the perfect place
for some summer lovin'!

*Available June 2007
wherever Harlequin books are sold.*

www.eHarlequin.com

HAR75169

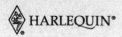

HARLEQUIN®

INTRIGUE®

COMING NEXT MONTH

#993 HIGH SOCIETY SABOTAGE by Kathleen Long
Bodyguards Unlimited, Denver, CO (Book 4 of 6)
In order to blend into the world of CEO Stephen Turner, PPS agent
Sara Montgomery adopts the role she left behind years ago—
debutante—to stop investors from dying.

#994 ROYAL LOCKDOWN by Rebecca York
Lights Out (Book 1 of 4)
A brand-new continuity! Princess Ariana LeBron brought the famous
Beau Pays sapphire to Boston, which security expert Shane Peters
intended to steal. But plans changed when an act of revenge plunged
Boston into a complete blackout.

#995 COLBY VS. COLBY by Debra Webb
Colby Agency: The Equalizers (Book 3 of 3)
Does the beginning of the Equalizers mean the end of the Colby
Agency? Jim Colby and Victoria Camp-Colby go head-to-head when
they both send agents to L.A., where nothing is as simple as it seems.

#996 SECRET OF DEADMAN'S COULEE by B.J. Daniels
Whitehorse, Montana
A downed plane in Missouri Breaks badlands was bad enough. But on
board was someone who was murdered thirty-two years ago? Sheriff
Carter Jackson and Eve Bailey thought their reunion would be hard
enough....

#997 SHOWDOWN WITH THE SHERIFF by Jan Hambright
Sheriff Logan Brewer called Rory Matson back to Reaper's Point, not
to identify her father's body, but the skull discovered in his backpack
at the time of his death.

#998 FORBIDDEN TEMPTATION by Paula Graves
Women were dying in Birmingham's trendy nightclub district, and only
Rose Browning saw a killer's pattern emerging. But she didn't know
how to stop him, not until hot-shot criminal profiler Daniel Hartman
arrived.

www.eHarlequin.com

HICNM0507